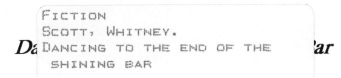

"Whitney Scott has written a deeply moving and finely wrought novel about the true voices families use amongst themselves: in silence, in pain, in joy, and in the smallest mercies shared. Her characters become our own mother, father, brother and sister.

"Searingly honest, and yet full of immense compassion ... *Dancing to the End of the Shining Bar* is about the continual, all-encompassing journey to an understanding of who we are and what our deepest graces in life are — courage, endurance and love.

"Whitney Scott's novel nourishes us, our deepest roots in this passionate work full of rollicking humor and almost unendurable pathos. So memorable is this family in the throes of uneasy transformation that we liken them to our own."

— Denise Chávez
acclaimed author of *Last of the Menu Girls,*
The Woman Who Knew the Language of the Animals and
Face of an Angel

Dancing
to the
End of the
Shining Bar

a novel
by
Whitney Scott

Outrider Press
Crete, Illinois

Sections of this novel have been previously published in *Wide Open Magazine* and *The Star.*

Library of Congress Catalog Card Number 93-086798

Front cover photograph by John Thoeming
Back cover photograph by C. S. Kaczmarczyk
Cover design by Salvatore Concialdi

ISBN 0-9621039-2-6
SAN 250-4057

PRINTED IN THE UNITED STATES OF AMERICA

Acknowledgements

Thanks to Karen Darr, Beverly Dudey, C.S. Kaczmarczyk, Susan Latham, Marion Stern, Fran Zell and, of course, Denise Chávez.

Contents

To come to what you do not know,
you must go by the way you do not know.

— St. John of the Cross

Dancing
to the
End of the
Shining Bar

June, 1985 — INTRIGUE

*I*ntrigue and terror mingle inside me. In front of us a long stretch of shining nickel bar angles towards the right, disappearing from our range of vision so that I can barely make out a tantalizing segment of neatly-trimmed, short red-blonde curls across the bar, brown eyes, a warm smile and a thin, gold chain around a slender neck surrounded by an ivory silk blouse. I keep glancing in that direction, wishing she would look my way, dreading that she might.

"Hey, Lucy," my brother Rick says, regaining my attention, "Did you know this is the original 1920 bar from Murphy's Tavern?" He holds his vodka stinger. He'd never heard of the drink until we went to see "Company" and heard the song about the ladies who lunched and drank them. After the show, we'd stopped off to see flamenco dancing performed by a friend of mine, Esperanza Cortez, born Rachel Feinstein in Highland Park. Rick had absent-mindedly groped for the name of the drink, asking the bartender for "A vodka, uh, a vodka bite, uh, a snapper."

"How 'bout a vodka prick?" the blue-eyed, bearded boy had answered suggestively. For at least a year after that my brother drank only stingers; now he rarely drinks at all.

9

Stingers are currently reserved for festive occasions. Today's stinger marks just such an event — a 30-day, unbroken string of relatively stable blood tests, a day to celebrate, with the possibility that he can return to his job as an administrator with the Department of Housing and Urban Development, at least on a part-time basis. Even the notorious Chicago climate cooperates, giving us a beautiful spring day, rare this late in June.

The jukebox plays the opening narrative of Noel Coward's "Mad About the Boy" and as Barbara Cook gives five syllables to the opening word of the song, singing "Ma-aa-a-a-ad a-butt the bo-o-oy," Rick catches my eye and says, "I'm sure Noel was."

"Was what?"

"Mad about the boy. It was supposed to be some movie star, you know, somebody famous in the 'forties."

"No. I didn't."

"Well, it was." He sips his drink, reflected in the bar's shining surface.

"Want to dress up as 'forties characters for the party? I'd like to be Bogey," I say. "But I don't think I can talk with a lit cigarette dangling from my lip. Besides, I can't see without my glasses anymore."

"That's all right, Lucy," he says, smiling wickedly, resplendent in his new gray blazer, freshly-trimmed dark curls framing his deep-set, dark eyes. "With me done up as Lauren Bacall, no one will notice."

He stops, his attention caught by something I can't see, something over my shoulder.

"Someone's looking at you, Lucy. Don't look up," he says, a note of excitement in his voice.

"Get serious. Now really, who should we be?" It's been a few years since we've come up with costumes and gone to one of Fran's infamous Independence Day parties together. One year we went as a matching washer and dryer with circular doors that opened out, mine revealing whites in the wash cycle and his, brightly colored towels being fluffed and dried. Not only was it difficult to dance in those large, spray-painted cardboard boxes, we'd almost gotten into a fight while making them, with me insisting on no less than three coats of spray paint on all viewable surfaces, even the inside surface of the doors. Rick protested a coat more or less on the doors' interiors wasn't that important, but I finally convinced him by reminding him we were, after all, top quality appliances.

"Who we go as would depend on the theme," he answers, "but Lucy, someone's looking —"

"It's called 'Get in the Spirit,' this year," I remind him. "Leaves us plenty of room for creativity. We could be the Spirit of St. Louis. Do you want to be a bi-plane?"

"I want you to listen to me and believe me when I tell you someone's looking at you because she was before and she's looking at you now."

"Okay, Rick. Who?" I ask. Clearly, he's not going to give up.

"The blonde you were cruising." He gives me a half-smile.

"I wasn't cruising. And she's a redhead."

"Right. The one you weren't cruising isn't cruising you right back." I find my chin lifting and turning around toward her. "I said don't look up. She's cute. Classic features. Beautiful, almost." He smiles, turning to me. "Not only attractive, but intelligent-looking, too." He glances briefly at her. "She's watching us and smiling. A very pretty smile. A

11

bright smile. I'm going to leave for a minute so she can come
talk to you."

"She won't, for God's sake!" I can't imagine anyone I
find appealing coming over to me even though it's happened
on occasion. It's hard to think it could take place now,
though, so soon after the break-up with Christina. Sometimes
I've been the initiator of a split, the dumper, relieved except
for the twinges of loneliness and guilt that have invariably
attacked. This was especially true years ago when I divorced
my husband, Ed. Other times, I've been the dumpee in a
break-up, feeling unattractive, unwanted and, occasionally,
beyond help. Since Christina left me, my feelings have ranged
from stoic self-discipline on occasion to wretched despair
much of the time. One night I even thought about loading my
pistol. Rick knows I have it but that's all I'll tell him. No
one else even suspects I own a gun. And certainly no one
knows it's hidden in the freezer behind the ice cubes.

"So you go talk to her, Lucy. After all, you look good!
Your hair's great, you're wearing your new earrings, who
knows what could happen?" Rick glances her way again.

"Isn't she with someone?" I shift on my bar stool,
glancing in the polished mirror over the bar to check my face,
pushing my long, loose brunette curls from my face to show
off my dark eyes and ivory complexion.

"Hard to say, even though I can see further around than
you can. But there are people sitting next to her and one
woman standing just to the side. The one who's standing is
attractive, too." He pauses, considering with a seasoned eye.
"Switch seats with me so you can see more. After all, you're
a reporter, Lucy. Size her up. So who cares if she's with
someone? Let her decide."

"Who?"

"The blonde who's a redhead at the end of the bar."

"I couldn't." My inner shyness still gets the upper hand. That's especially true lately. Still, my eyes meet her glance briefly in the mirror, a small rush of adrenaline reflecting itself in the smile I send her way.

"What — you couldn't? You, who have been known to find someone in a bar in less than two minutes?"

"Rick! Stop exaggerating."

He grins, proudly. After all, who taught me? "Who's exaggerating? What about that little brunette from New Orleans? That was more like ten seconds." He sees my look, backs down. "All right, all right, make that 30 seconds and the next thing I knew, the two of you were slow dancing, staring into each other's eyes and you were trying to remember your college French." He laughs into his drink, remembering. "You almost went home with her. An hour after meeting her."

I remember. Michelle, with dark eyes, a small, compact body and a contagious laugh. Her lips on my neck as we danced, clung, in the darkest corner of the bar. Her last night in town and I find her. Why do I always seem to find them on their last nights? Before returning home from vacation? Before moving back in with their mothers? Before getting married? Before reconciling with estranged lovers? Before moving 220 miles away? Before undergoing religious conversions and seeing me as an occasion of sin?

"She was staying with friends," I tell Rick. He stares silently at our reflections in the mirror over the bar, so I continue, "and called me that morning at 5:00." This memory elicits a knot of grief in my stomach — for Michelle or Christina? — so it takes a moment before I go on. "She said she couldn't stop thinking about me."

13

Dancing to the End . . . .

Still no response from Rick. I wonder where he's drifting. The music is vintage Beatles, wanting to hold my hand. After a couple of sips, I return to my story.

"I called her when she got back to New Orleans but she said she had to whisper so her roommate wouldn't overhear."

"Roommate. Yeah. I've heard that one."

"Yeah."

"No, Luce, you did the right thing. Just as well you didn't go home with her when you didn't know her."

I look down at the bar napkin with the damp circles. "Really only did that once, years ago."

"And didn't you wind up going out with her — what was her name, Jodie?" I nod. "For months afterward?" Again, I nod. "Typical," he says, smiling wryly.

I laugh. "Maybe just more monogamous than you are."

"Not a tough record to beat." He sighs, maybe thinking of the many men he's had sex with, the friends, lovers, tricks and fuck-buddies, some dead now, maybe recalling the few who mattered. I sense us drifting into regrets about the past, not a good direction for either of us, especially not now, not for me.

"Well, serial monogamy hasn't worked any wonders for me," I say, my thoughts returning yet again to Christina, the beguiling woman I'd met right after breaking up with Linda. Seems like years ago, though it's only been a few months.

Questioningly, I look at him. "Maybe I never should have left Linda. She was solid and steady." My brother gives me a look. "She was neat and clean and kept her garage swept out." He rolls his eyes in disbelief. Feebly, I add, "She was a great cook and ironed her sheets." He shakes his head, laughing.

I protest, trying to keep a straight face. "She's a good woman, Rick."

"So's Mother Teresa. Face it; you've always liked them bad and beautiful."

He's right and I'm laughing at myself right along with him when he sighs, very deeply this time, turning serious and thoughtful.

"You knew she was bad news the minute you met her," he says softly in a concerned voice, looking down into his drink.

"Who?" I ask, knowing very well who he means.

"Christina."

"Oh. Maybe. Yeah."

"Definitely." He gazes at his reflection in the shiny bar. "Definitely bad and definitely beautiful."

"Yes. Beautiful." Sighing, memories of her flood my senses. She had come at me a shard at a time from across the room, fragmenting, shifting picture planes dressed in a multi-colored pants suit, looking like she'd collided with a Sicilian pizza truck — but magnificent. Everything about Christina — the graceful sway of her tall, thin body, her long, blonde-gray hair tied up to reveal a slender neck, that carefully taut smile as she'd extended those slim, sensitive fingers in a cool handshake — had silently beckoned me with her unspoken message: "Rescue me." Of course, I'd tried.

And failed.

At least it hadn't taken long though it seems like we shared a lifetime together in those few months.

It hurts to recall the tilt of Christina's head as she'd looked at me briefly, glancing away toward the trees in the distance, then back to me. "There's part of me that wants to be with you so much but I know I can't," she'd told me less than a month ago and I'd trembled in the warm spring sun.

I lifted my head to face her. She was regarding me intently. "What I wanted most," I said, in a voice from deep inside that I rarely heard myself use, "was to wake up with the sun coming into my room. To look across at the other side of the bed and see your face there beside me — not just on an occasional weekend but for a lifetime." Tears welled up in me. Christina touched my hair. Her own eyes were full.

"That's exactly my point, Lucy," she said. "This has been an erotic friendship for me, but it's gotten to be a lot more than that for you. You're in too deep already."

"But it could grow for you, too, if you'd give it a chance," I said. "How do you know what it could come to mean for you if you don't try?"

"You're just not the right person for me," she said. Mute then, she shook her head.

Stabbing pains in my gut, in my head. "Why, Christina," I said, my voice a thin howl, reminding me of the night sounds in the mountains of Taos. "For God's sake, why not me?"

No answer, just a turning away of those deep gray eyes, gray-green now in the sun as she seemed to study the trees. Amazing how many trees there are in Lincoln Park, in the middle of a huge city. Sighing, she returned her gaze to me.

I leaned toward her, demanding, "I deserve an answer!"

"I don't want to!" Christina said, black darts shooting from her eyes. "I can't stay with people who are like me! There's too much of the ups and downs, the craziness. You're not just a reporter; you're a poet, a serious writer and you're all over the place, emotionally." She stopped, sniffing, eyes brimming. "I'll erase the memories of us together. I'll wipe them out with other people, people I couldn't ever care about, people as different from you as possible."

16

My stomach revulsed at the thought of Christina in other women's arms. I turned away from her but she caught my face in her hands, forcing me to look at her.

Her faced loomed closer, boring in her message: "I've worked hard, very hard, to build some stability in my life," she said. "I'm a dancer, a choreographer and I can't get involved with another artist. It's too intense."

Too intense. Too much of the ups and downs, the powerful highs I needed to nourish me. I sobbed, shoulders shaking in the morning light filtering through the trees. Again, again and yet again I had been found to be too intense, too spiritual, too artistic, too much of a visionary, too scary, just plain too much.

*　*　*　*　*

"Nothing like the wet blanket of memory," Rick says as though reading my thoughts, quickly veering away from his own. He glances again at the reddish-blonde curls at the end of the shining bar, moving into action.

"Let's dance." He takes my hand and we rise together.

*　*　*　*　*

Some years before in the middle of the heat-filled midwestern summer, we had decided to learn some new dances. We were both ending long-term relationships and had spent a lot of time together, sometimes with Julie, who was still my little girl then, other times just the two of us, framing old photos, going to art galleries and book stores, visiting the friends we had together and trying to make more. Since I'd been writing for a big daily paper then, I could afford to treat us both to a Saturday afternoon disco dance class for adults at the local community college.

The boy teacher, barely 18 with long, dark blonde hair, wore baggy, striped pants with a black shirt half unbuttoned. The girl was pretty and fine featured, with pale blonde hair tied back with a red ribbon, in black tights and a red shirt tied tightly into a knot at her waist. The room was crowded with two dozen wary-looking men in dark dress slacks and short-sleeved shirts, accompanied by women in slacks and denim jeans, some so tight you could see the panty lines beneath the stretched blue fabric. Rick and I were in our bar clothes, dressed to dance. He had on one of the long-sleeved, cotton plaid shirts he liked to wear to the bars, half-unbuttoned and with sleeves rolled up, because it showed off his body-builder's physique that way. His tan pants were so tight anyone who was sufficiently interested could tell he wore no underwear. My beige silk blouse was unbuttoned as much as decency allowed, with black jeans, cowboy boots and no bra.

The carpeted room was dark except for the small, raised stage area where the teachers stood in the white spotlight. First the girl spoke into the microphone introducing herself, explaining that a single step and its variations would form the basis of the afternoon's lesson. The boy said his name into the mike in a deep baritone voice, adding that variations allowed for individual creativity.

Moving to the front of the stage, they demonstrated a sort of grapevine step, left leg crossing in front of the right and back, then right leg crossing behind the left, followed by a little dip and a quick side-step in between. First the boy, then the girl, turning left, turning right. Then the two together, eyes not meeting, two bodies separated in space but both moving exactly on beat, the sounds of the Supremes' "Baby

Love" washing over us from two large speakers. After the first chorus, the boy occasionally threw in an extra little move with his shoulders or arms. The girl glared at him disapprovingly and he returned to the simpler routine.

"That's enough of the golden oldies sound," the boy said in a businesslike manner as the music stopped abruptly. Now it was our turn as we divided into two lines, partner facing partner in the darkened silence. Slowly the girl counted the beats evenly, the human equivalent of a drum beat, while the boy reminded us of our crosses and dips.

The people in my line took their partners' left hands in their right, faltering through the step. To the left, slowly. To the right. Twice to the left, twice to the right, faster, and with increasing speed came more energy, verve and spontaneity.

The girl put on an album and we crossed and dipped more fluidly yet. The couple toward the left had been doing fairly well until the music had been added, but the 50-ish, balding man began tripping and sweating, apparently in his effort to keep up with the beat, his head shiny and moist in the half-light. It didn't help when the boy added some arm and shoulder movements, which seemed to make the sweaty man's balance more precarious. As long as Rick and I didn't try to cover too much ground, we did reasonably well. We were used to dancing together in the gay bars. A man dancing with a woman sometimes raised a few eyebrows as well as hackles in such places but that didn't discourage us.

The dance class was more dimly lit than some of the bars we went to and that was fine with me, since I had no particular desire to distinguish the features of the people moving all around us. We were there to learn, not socialize with people who were so different from Rick and me.

Dancing to the End ....

The girl showed us how to throw a spin into the basic step, which I liked, so I used a lot of them, spinning left and right, forward and backward. Rick and I were enjoying the pounding music and motion, spinning along in our own little world. We were camping it up in gay bar fashion, flinging our heads and arms outrageously, when Rick stopped suddenly, freeze-framed in the exaggerated pose of a high-fashion model, chin thrust up in haughty grandeur, the stereotype of the quintessential gay queen. Some couples paused in their dancing, glancing our way. The balding man tripped into me.

His partner, tall and slender in a pink pants suit, frowned, whispering, "Pardon." She said loudly to the man who was recovering his balance, "That man — you know, you're right — I think he's that way. God knows why they're here." She resolutely led him away from us across the room.

Her prejudiced remark, so cruel and unnecessary, stunned me. I stopped moving. Rick grabbed my elbow, leaning over to look at my face. His own was pale, with patches of color at the top of his cheek bones. "Are you okay? Do you want to leave?" he asked.

Before I could answer, he leaned in closer to me and said distinctly, "Fuck them, Lucy, let's dance!"

Eyes were staring at us, some from the stage. The music stopped in the middle of a chorus and the boy, who'd apparently been observing our little soap opera, said into the microphone, "Let's cool off. Take ten."

"Something cold to drink?" Rick asked, glancing at the soft drink machine in the corner. He turned and glided to it, adding a little dip, spin and toss of his head.

*   *   *   *   *

20

The sweaty man and his dance partner returned, he tight-lipped and grim, sweatier than ever, apparently the result of non-stop practice during the ten-minute break. The woman kept whispering hoarsely, "Just remember to count. *ONE,* two, three, four, five, six, seven, EIGHT." The boy and girl called the class back to the room.

Less than one minute into the next dance, the girl had reviewed all we'd learned so far and was demonstrating new combinations when the boy teacher surprised me from behind by cutting in and grabbing my hand purposefully. My first instinct was to withdraw in fear, since I was feeling outcast. He smiled though and I liked his dark eyes and the way his long, blonde hair swung as he moved. He was easy to follow and Rick, who encouraged from the sidelines, moved to the rhythm and threw a nod in my direction from time to time.

The blonde boy didn't speak. I was grateful for that since I sometimes tense up with strangers in social settings and the last thing I wanted to hear was a man telling me to relax. He danced fluidly, occasionally catching my eye, showing me a new routine with the hands and arms. It was easy to mirror his moves, so completely, yet so subtly did he communicate them to me. I relaxed my concentration, felt it loosen and give way, let myself go with the music, moving surely, easily with the boy whose hair flared, catching and reflecting the dim light in the room. My assurance grew with each pulsing musical phrase, each beat that carried me forward into new levels of confidence. Our cross-overs, spins and twists seemed to occur simultaneously as the boy sent me signals I felt rather than saw. In response, I stamped my own small mark on these themes and variations, returning them subtly altered, encouraging him to work his creative changes in turn. The boy moved with increasing verve, emanating brightness and

21

energy. He flashed me a smile of genuine joy, delighted at my obvious pleasure and progress, exhilarated for my ease.

Rick clapped as the music ended. "Hey, you two really looked good," he said, taking my hand as the boy gave me a warm smile of authentic appreciation, nodded slightly and walked across the room. "Let's try that."

After the lesson we went to my house, set the window air conditioner on "High" and moved a coffee table and chair from the living room to clear a practice space. Julie, who couldn't have been more than 12 or 13 then, sat on the top step of the stairs, leaning against the wall and propping her right leg through the wrought iron bannister.

"I gotta see this," she said, grinning, running her fingers through her long, straight hair. "You two doin' new steps."

"You just wait, you'll be learning from us," Rick said, but I realized he wasn't as confident as he sounded when he added, "I'll bet you didn't set the table yet, Julie. Why don't you go in the kitchen and do that now?"

"I can still lean around the corner and check this out," she said, gathering her long legs under her as she rose.

"Never mind, Rick. We'll be her comic relief for the day," I said, going through records. "What about some classic Benny Goodman? Think that's about our vintage?"

He stood next to me, disgruntled, looking at albums. "We really should organize these some day so we can find things."

"What makes you think I can't already? Or want to?"

No answer, just a barely audible grunt from the back of his throat then, "Julie, have you got any good dance music?"

No answer there either. But she reappeared in a minute with two albums which she tossed on the couch. "Try these. But I gotta watch. If you guys have any good moves, I'll show Kim tomorrow when I go to her house."

Our efforts were filled mostly with false starts so that Julie gave up on the hope of learning anything useful and disappeared into her room. But slowly, as we supplemented her rock albums with a few classics from our own youth, Rick and I managed better and better until we were moving easily on beat to the music. Even though the sun was setting, we didn't stop to turn on lights. Instead, we swayed in the multi-colored glow cast by the antique stained glass which hung in the picture window and we danced, spinning, dipping and crossing over without effort, feeling the beat and power of the Supremes singing, "Ain't No Mountain High Enough," making us feel it, making us know it and believe it right along with them as Diana Ross' voice soared over the horns.

There is only one essential for weightlessness, no matter what the national space agency tells us. It cannot be planned, practiced or bestowed, nor can it be the result of any training, however rigorous. It is the spontaneous, total and willing suspension of disbelief, given instinctively from some inner impulse that propels our best selves. It is the faith-filled energy that keeps time with some universal tide, stops time, is time, blurring distinctions between one being and another, one moment and another, one light source and another. And so we danced in the shifting, stained-glass light, lightly, moving in unison without so much as glancing at each other, but feeling the moves together, rising, weightless with the energy of vast cadences. We were one and free, neither awake nor dreaming, undisturbed by time and its constraints, and more than that we knew it with a blissful awareness that we were meshed, part of an eternal rhythm of the cosmic dance.

*   *   *   *   *

23

"C'mon, you be Ginger Rogers and we'll do it like the pros," Rick whispers hoarsely, throwing me into a dramatic back bend, leaning me over a shining nickel bar stool as I catch a glimpse of our reflection in the polished mirror. I respond fluidly, as though I'd been expecting that move. It can't be the result of alcohol-induced relaxation, since I've been drinking nothing but sparkling water with a twist. Might as well welcome the sensation, though. So I rub my leg against his, up along the outside of his hip and fling my right arm out, arching my back in pseudo-passion.

He takes his cue, further arching his back and neck, flinging his hair in the dramatic manner of Rudolph Valentino and I fall into my Theda Bara vamp imitation, throatily stage whispering, "Kiss me-ee-ee, my fo-oo-ool." No one in the bar can ignore us. We combine elements of boogie-woogie, the Charleston and a camp Apache dance, when suddenly Rick switches into a semi-staid, eight-inches-away, no-body-parts-touching, series of box steps, dancing me soberly to the end of the shining bar. He touches the redhead on the arm and says with a straight face, "Hi. This is my sister. She'd like to dance with you," smiles charmingly and disappears in the direction of the men's room.

July, 1985 — BRING YOUR OWN FOOD

$\mathcal{S}$ince 1942, Aunt Hazel's come to my mother's house every two or three days for free meals. But until she'd arrived a minute ago, the family hadn't seen her in a week.

She's still angry because we ate our family Sunday dinner without her last week. For the last few weeks we've been eating this meal when Rick feels like it, sometime around the middle of the day but not necessarily when the clock strikes noon. It's easier on my mother, too. She's tired and worn out, not so much from extra errands and trips to the doctors' offices as from her endless worrying and fretting over Rick, the many night she spends praying for him in the dark, saying rosary after rosary.

So that's the tradition we're trying to vary now; no more noon Sunday dinners cast in stone, not unless it just happens to work out that way. Though she's protested this, it's in Mother's best interests, since she refuses any help in her kitchen, claiming no one else can work there.

Hazel can't adjust to the changes the family's made. Months ago, she wouldn't accept the fact that Rick could no longer help her hang drapes or move furniture onto her porch for the summer, things he'd helped with for years. She reminded him and nagged at him until finally, Arty, Rick's dad and my stepfather, told her there was no way Rick could do it. She even asked my mother and Arty if they would help her, which is ridiculous with their heart conditions. She misses the long visits with my mother, often cut short when Rick is in the hospital. She complains that the phone is tied up more often now, making it harder to call.

Certainly, she knows my brother is sick, but Ma gave her some story about "asthmatic bronchitis" so Hazel doesn't know Rick is dying. She can't see the reason to have the household routines vary according to his needs. This change in the Sunday family dinner ritual is too much for her.

Last week, she ran up the stairs from the front door just as Mother was putting the dishes away. When Hazel walked into the kitchen and saw that dinner was over, she refused to fix herself a plate, refused to sit down, refused to even take off her coat; she just stood there, complete with thickly-pencilled Joan Crawford eyebrows, dressed in her plastic rain bonnet and spotless white rain coat, screaming at Mother, "I won't be treated this way — to have to sit and eat alone — alone, like a dog!"

"You won't be alone, Hazel. I'll sit with you," Arty offered in a rare show of sociability, but she wouldn't budge.

"This is how you treat your oldest friend, closer to you than a sister?" The arched, pencilled eyebrows disappeared beneath her bangs of perfectly frosted hair.

Mother didn't even make an attempt. She was too tired to care, disheveled-looking in an old skirt and blouse worn under her apron and I didn't have the motivation to bother.

Hazel's not really an aunt. She's a neighbor who grew up with my mother and lost her husband to World War II combat. Mother, who's always had a hard time making friends, more or less adopted this childhood friend into the family. Although she knows everyone in the neighborhood,

"Skinny Skinflint" Hazel doesn't have many friends, since most people won't put up with her, partly because of her renowned stinginess. She also insists that her needs and wants be given instant priority and the temper tantrums she throws when she's not being catered to are legendary in these twelve square blocks of immigrant steel workers and their children. When Rick and I were kids, the neighborhood was mainly Polish, with a sprinkling of Slavs; now, many of the tiny corner stores have signs in both Spanish and English.

Anyway, Hazel was furious last week and isn't much better now. Rick's having a fine day, so Sunday dinner is on time when Hazel arrives; She knocks, letting herself in the unlocked door; climbing the steep stairs quickly and silently, she carries a large paper sack from Burger King. The bag's greasy smell clashes with the homemade food aromas that help warm Mother's large, eat-in kitchen. I stare. Hazel hasn't spent money on restaurant food in years.

When her boyfriend, Jack, a local hood, dropped dead of a heart attack early one morning in their living room, he left over $350,000 in large bills stuffed into a variety of shoe boxes. Hazel immediately crammed $9,950 into each of 36 small paper bags, jamming the small bags into one good-sized shopping bag. Then she called Mother for help. Together, they rode the bus into Chicago, starting separate accounts for Hazel in ten different banks. The tenth turned out to be the last, since it happened to be offering a special promotion at the time — a free safety deposit box for starting a new account. Triumphantly, Hazel hid the rest of the cash in it.

"They don't check on cash deposits under $10,000. That way, his kids will never get their hands on it," Hazel gloated.

It was cold and windy that day in November, but Hazel stood on Michigan Avenue insisting they didn't have the time to stop for lunch or a hot cup of coffee. It wasn't the time. "Skinflint" comes by her name honestly and she didn't want to go to a restaurant and pay for food. That afternoon, back at her house, she fixed tea and toast for Mother, then called the police, saying Jack had died while she'd been out shopping. That was six years ago. His children never got the money and Hazel hoards her riches.

One Sunday last winter, when she thought she'd lost the keys to her Cadillac DeVille, Hazel had emptied her purse all over Ma's kitchen table. From her designer brown lizard bag spilled several bobby pins, a couple of small safety pins, what appeared to be the keys to six safety deposit boxes on a key chain and an engraved money clip that had belonged to Jack. A $100 bill was visible in it, with at least two dozen other bank notes folded thickly beneath that. She also had two lipsticks, face powder, blush, mascara, eye shadow, a purse-sized spray bottle of "My Sin," a ballpoint pen marked "Ruzzo for State Rep" and several used tissues. There was a long, thin, clear plastic pill box with Elavil, Valium, Digitalis and three-quarters of a thickly-rolled joint. Finally, there were the car keys, her reduced-price senior citizen's bus pass and her ID for the federally subsidized senior lunch program. Mother had chided her about eating food other senior citizens genuinely needed and Hazel had launched into a tirade about being entitled and never getting to eat out anywhere else.

That's apparently changed today since she's obviously been out to Burger King.

"Hello," she mutters, entering the kitchen and shifting the fast food bag from hand to hand for emphasis. "I'll eat in the TV room. You're already sitting." She hangs her linen purse on the back of a chair and tugs at her matching peach-colored linen dress, briefly revealing a lace-trimmed ivory slip.

"Hazel, Hazel, there's room, there's always room for you. Just sit at your place." Mother's invariably had lots of patience with her, but cuts discussion short today, pointedly failing to inquire about her friend's week-long absence. She's brooding, probably because she's been haranguing me about my daughter, her only grandchild. My "little Julie" has been asserting her teenage independence by spending the entire summer with her father's family on the north side of Chicago, removing herself from us and our concerns. Not only that, she's going to be starting college in a few weeks, with only three days at our home for packing and farewells.

Mother and Arty were dead set against her going to Georgetown University, saying their "little Julie" was too young to be in Washington, D.C., so far from home. Despite the distance, I'm delighted for her opportunity, since I could never have afforded such an education for her on my modest income. Fortunately, Julie's worked the last two summers, has a grant as well as a scholarship and her father and I manage the rest.

Ed's always believed in the wisdom of investing in knowledge and isn't complaining about Julie's college costs though he's shouldered heavy responsibilities since marrying a woman with two boys of her own. Even when our daughter was little, Ed never bought her a toy that wasn't educational and rarely spent any time with her that didn't have as its goal some academic lesson, whether or not she was interested. The most casual walks after supper were turned into nature hikes as he leafed through his well-thumbed wildflower guide and bird book, attempting to identify anything he saw.

Although I'll miss Julie, it's frankly a relief not to be responsible for a tumultuous college-age daughter in the middle of this turmoil surrounding my brother's illness. But

Dancing to the End   . . . .

I grieve her leaving, frightened by the increasing distances of all types between us and wondering if she's irretrievably growing away. Despite the difficulties of raising her as a single, gay mother, I've never regretted fighting Ed for her custody. She is my daughter, bone of my bone, even now as she retreats from us, from me, really, into the shelter of Ed's more socially-acceptable, conventional lifestyle. I miss little Julie with a yearning that sometimes borders on anguish, fearing she may be lost to me forever.

Cowboy, the large silver and black dog that Rick adopted two years ago, comes skidding into the kitchen. He's 80 pounds of Malamute, Husky and wolf, with a long, shaggy tail, sharp, intelligent yellow eyes and an alert, but not menacing, air. Rick called him "Cowboy" because he was dating one of the leather cowboys from Halsted Street at the time. The dog's basically a sweet and obedient animal, with the goal of becoming a lap dog. When my brother feels up to it, he can still pick Cowboy up and hug him and the dog loves it, but most people are afraid of this quiet animal. Maybe they're put off by his leather collar with the chrome spikes.

"Here comes that damn wolf, messing up all my papers," Ma complains, sharply exhaling in exasperation.

Whether Rick's at home or in the hospital, every Saturday afternoon Mother cleans the floors. As she has done each weekend for decades, she starts with vacuuming the bedrooms and hallways, progresses to scrubbing the tiled floors in both bathrooms and finishes in the kitchen, washing the linoleum there. After she's done cleaning, Mother puts newspapers down all over the kitchen floor. That's the way things are done, the way they've always been done, down to the weekly ritual of cookies and coffee after the papers have been carefully arranged on the linoleum "to keep it nice."

30

Polish rugs as they are called, can only be fresh newspapers, which usually means that sooner or later Arty hollers at my mother, "Rae! Rae Ann! Where's the weekend paper? Where's my sports section? You didn't put it on the floor again, did you?" He knows very well that she has.

Mother stands, hands on hips in the kitchen doorway, glaring at Arty in the living room recliner. "So?" she asks, "So go and look if you're so concerned," and he rattles the latest issue of *Sports Illustrated* in irritation. How Mother can put up with him is beyond me. Granted, Arty proved to be a workable second husband for her years ago when she was a young widow with a small daughter, just as she proved invaluable to him, a neighborhood widower working at one of the steel mills and trying to raise his little boy. So they made a marriage and Rick and I blended into brother and sister.

And Arty did have a point — those newspapers on the floor were hazardous. When we were little, Rick and I would invariably come running into the kitchen, only to wind up skidding across the room, arms waving dramatically, loving the thrill of the forward momentum. Arty would finally gather up the papers after dinner time each Sunday when he could no longer live without the sports section or couldn't endure hearing us slide repeatedly into the refrigerator, whichever came first.

Respectable people in the neighborhood never kept the papers down past the middle of the afternoon on Sunday anyway, since friends and relatives used to drop in then, the men and boys in bright bow ties, suspenders and starched white shirts, the women and girls in their Sunday, flowered dresses and patent leather shoes. The girls' shoes had little straps that buckled over the ruffled, thin white socks, while the women wore pumps and nylons. If a man wore a belt along with his suspenders, Rick and I knew we couldn't trust him. That's what Mother always said.

In those days when we were kids and people used to pay Sunday visits, Mother made us stay in our good church clothes until 6 p.m. Rick and I would snack and play cards with everyone else but I hated wearing a dress, especially frilly things with stiff, scratchy, ruffles, and we missed Saturday's slides across the kitchen and the cheerful sound of the newspapers crumpling under our feet, leaving bare spots of floor exposed.

It was darkly rumored that Arty's sister, Sophie, who never had people over, kept her papers down until Tuesday, since she hated to throw anything away. I used to envy her two little boys, who had three days of sliding each week, whenever Aunt Sophie's back was turned.

Now it's Cowboy skidding, all four legs rigid as he collides into Hazel, knocking her against the table and sniffing the greasy Burger King bag hopefully. For a moment, Hazel teeters on her open-toe spike heels, but grabs the table edge and remains upright against it, however precariously.

"Dammit, Rae Ann, when are you going to get those papers off the floor, before somebody kills themselves?" Arty yells. Apparently overcome by the unaccustomed smells of fast food, the dog, who is usually so quiet and well-trained, jumps up on Hazel, who is stiff with fear.

Hazel grasps her paper bag protectively but realizes that she hasn't got hold of the table, just the table pads, which are sliding off the table top as she struggles to remain standing, buckling under the big dog's weight. The glasses, mercifully empty, topple over as the utensils and platters of food start their slide toward Hazel's immaculate linen dress.

She screams, "Your wolf, damn you, Rick! Your wolf is trying to attack me, to mutilate me! Is that what you want? My God, he's licking my face! And my hair!" Rick and Arty both grab the table pad, but part of me wishes they hadn't. I wouldn't mind seeing Hazel fall down with the potatoes and gravy on the Sunday papers. Mother turns to stare, face reddening and mouth clamped tight.

"Cowboy, get down. Don't terrorize people with love, honey," Rick says softly to the shaggy animal which drops down to all fours and goes to Rick's chair without a sound.

"My God, Rick, how you can stand to have that savage wolf in the house, I'll never, never know," Hazel says, becoming more shrill. "You wait and see, someday he's going to maim somebody, take off their arm and then you'll be sorry. You'll have yourself such a lawsuit! It's only that I'm such a good friend that I don't sue you. Anyone else would! Don't just stare at me, Rick. You should listen to me, but that's all right, because someday God's going to punish you, punish you bad, and then you'll know!" Rick shoots her a look of warning. Cowboy is his baby.

I can almost see Hazel's mind working, weighing the possible benefits and costs of continuing with her uproar, calculating the risk of a major confrontation with Rick. A shadow crosses her eyes, quickly becoming memory.

"I'll sit, just at a corner," Hazel mumbles, fluffing her hair and sliding onto one of the carved mahogany chairs that matches the table. No one speaks. She has decided to forego the battle as she straightens the table pad with precision and the air conditioner hums in the background, providing the only sound in the room.

Mother always protects the 25-year-old table top with its custom-made pads, but rarely bothers with a table cloth. I hate eating from dishes on top of the bare table pads. Though they're scrubbed thoroughly clean with cleanser, they make me feel somehow unfinished and queasy. I wouldn't mind eating off place mats or the unprotected table, not that Mother would ever hear of that, but I prefer a tablecloth. Rick always used a cloth when I ate at his house, priding himself on the attractive tables he set with sparkling silver, spot-free glassware and coordinating napkins carefully folded. That's when he had a table to set and his own house to set it in. But this is Mother's house and kitchen. She says I make needless work for myself, ironing so much.

"Why did you set such a table, when it's just us?" she asks whenever the family eats at my house.

"For God's sake, Ma, it's no big deal. It's just a permanent-press table cloth."

"With the matching napkins, too. No wonder you have such bursitis; it's from all that ironing. You didn't have bursitis when you lived home with me." I was 19 years younger then and there were a lot of things I didn't have at the time, including three gray hairs, an unconscious habit of grinding my teeth when I'm under pressure and a lily-of-the-valley tattoo on my left breast.

It's strange that Mother cares so little about the finer points, like tablecloths and napkins, yet she and Rick are so alike in many other ways.

I sit back watching the two of them, so sharp-featured and fine-skinned, smoothly-plumed twin eagles with their elegant high foreheads and cheekbones. Mother sits for a moment on the edge of the straight-backed chair near Rick's, her bony arms hunching over her knees which protrude like white-edged knobs covered with thin nylon mesh. They have always resembled each other, especially in profile. Mother had their portraits painted together about ten years ago, saying it was a mother and son picture and in every way that mattered, it was.

They are equally alike when it comes to their passion about food. The two of them can go on and on about the crispness of the caraway seeds in the rye bread, the amount of vitamin C in tomato juice as opposed to orange, the correct way to dribble melted cheese over vegetables and why no bread should be thawed in a microwave oven for more than two seconds.

Mother touches Rick's arm, fixing her eyes anxiously on his. "You'll eat now, won't you? You're going to eat?"

"Of course I'm going to eat. Can't wait," he says, smiling.

"That's good," she says, rising and moving toward the stove. "You know how important it is for you to eat."

Mother's policing of Rick eating or not-eating, or not-eating-enough-of-the-right-foods is really nothing new, but is simply an extension of the force-feeding she'd put us through as children. As a child in her house, I had often dreaded Ma at meal times, for I was an unenthusiastic eater and knew the tension that could bring.

Not so with Rick. From his first meeting with her when he was barely eight, Rick had welcomed the attention, asking shyly for second and even third helpings, basking in the warmth of her grateful smiles while I'd squirmed, trying to pick at the food as if I were eating.

It was at their first meeting, a Sunday meal together in Ma's big kitchen in the old house on Poplar Street, that Rick and Mother had fallen fully, irretrievably in love. They had looked at each other over the mounds of mashed potatoes and gravy, piles of broiled chicken carefully seasoned with sage and basil, baskets of hot, homemade biscuits, steaming squares of lasagna dripping pale cheese tendrils and the cut glass bowl brimming with lush chunks of tomatoes, carrots, green peppers and three kinds of lettuce. That pale, skinny little boy of eight had smelled the apple slices warming in the oven and stared. He'd fixed his gaze on her with the coiled silences and longings locked away for two motherless years of canned soup, Twinkies and peanut butter sandwiches made with stale bread — and he smiled.

At first the corners of his lips had twitched, so that I wasn't sure if he was about to cry and maybe he wasn't, either. But the smile had won out, spreading over his face like the rivulets of melted butter cascading down the rounded mountain of tiny green peas in front of him.

He smiled for the two years of days and weeks and months of lonely meals, of changing the beds and doing the dishes alone, of the long, solitary hours spent drawing pictures in the house each day, for he saw an end to them now. He smiled for the tormented nights, receding already in his memory, of turning over restlessly on unironed sheets, dreaming for his lost mother, that dark, broodingly artistic soul he mirrored. When other boys might have been dreaming of outer space adventures and grand slam home runs, he'd dreamt of lost cleanliness and order, pans of lasagna carefully patterned with cheese and cut evenly into squares, neat rows of green beans topped with diagonally-sliced almonds.

When he smiled and looked into Mother's eyes, this scrawny, awkward boy who'd been dutifully hauled to Our Lady of the Sacred Heart Church every Sunday since his birth gazed at the big-boned, dark-haired, Polish woman and saw an angel, a replacement Mother who might guard him from the dark boisterousness of his father; she who would cut his sandwiches carefully into fourths before wrapping them and placing them lovingly in his lunch box with the apple and homemade peanut butter cookies; she who would be standing in the kitchen, waiting for him after school each day; she who would make him brush his teeth and pray for his dead mother's soul each night before tucking him in with a kiss.

I couldn't have known all this then. These were insights gleaned and glimpsed over our years of coming together as brother and sister, as he slowly came to tell me stories about his mother, once tall, graceful and darkly beautiful; so vibrantly alive, enacting scenes from favorite movies and creating small islands of beauty in their tiny, dingy frame house with her pastel drawings of meticulously arranged flowers, becoming wasted and shrivelled with the cancer that so quickly withered her and ended her life.

"Everything looks great. You fussed for us," Rick had told Mother that day on Poplar Street, never taking his intensely aged, eight-year-old eyes from her face. Mother glowed, first glancing briefly at the boy's father, lingering silently, hopefully in the kitchen doorway, then restoring her gaze to the frail little boy, her nervous hands still and soft for once. "I was glad to," she said. "You eat now. There's plenty, you'll see."

And he did.

* * * * *

"Hazel, if you're going to sit at the table, then sit next to us, not at the corner, for Heaven's sake." Arty is hungry and irritated. Turning in his chair, he tries to read the sports pages on the floor, but they are too far away to be read from the table this week. He sighs in resignation, a short, solid man with pale blue eyes that can still sparkle with enthusiasm. He

37

removes his eyeglasses, polishes them with the tail of his short-sleeved, plaid cotton shirt and replaces them with a small sound of satisfaction. Now he can see his food properly. Now he is ready to eat.

He glances at the old digital watch on his wrist, commenting, "There's a sale on men's watches at J.C. Penney. Think I'll go look at them after dinner." He's been saying this for years but not doing it, hating to replace his old Seiko. It had been the first of its kind 10 years ago, cumbersome and costly, almost $300, long ago supplanted by newer models that were smaller, lighter, sturdier and a fraction of the original expense. Arty buys everything twice; he's literally the first person on his block to own any new gadget or electronic toy that comes on the market, no matter what its price; then later, usually many years later, he grudgingly replaces for a few dollars what has become the dinosaur of its species.

Hazel slides the chair closer to the table, to the left of Rick and across from me.

Mother gets a large serving fork from a kitchen drawer. There's no sense in trying to help her since she refuses help in the kitchen though she lets Rick work there with her occasionally. She puts a dish of sliced roast beef down next to the baked chicken, cole slaw made from scratch, mashed potatoes, gravy, beets, Jell-O, peas and homemade pickles scored in decorative patterns with a fork.

"You did it again, Rae Ann! You made too much food!"

"Arty, I always make a side meat on Sunday and you know it." Ma has gone through this verbal food fight with Arty for 29 years. He invariably protests but consistently eats everything and usually downs seconds.

"Where's the bread?" he asks.

"God, we forgot it! It's still in the oven," Rick says, whirling around to the stove.

"Never mind, Rick, I've got it." Mother turns and grabs a damp dish towel from the sink and uses it as a pot holder on the hot metal pan of dinner rolls. It sputters and steams against the burning aluminum, searing the air with the pan's hot metallic smell.

"Don't grab a hot pan with a wet towel, Rae. The heat goes right through the wetness. Use a pot holder, for God's sake, before you burn yourself."

"I'm using the towel and I am *not* burning myself. I'm perfectly fine," Ma says in a warning tone that even Arty respects. He's the first to grab a roll when she puts them on the table. Rick's already started on his Jell-O and a chicken leg. He ignores Hazel, who's making a major production out of opening the Burger King bag with much crackling and crunching of paper.

"You have to bring your own food to get a decent meal around here," she says cuttingly, as she removes with elaborately large gestures one regular burger, one small fries and a small coffee, placing each item on her plate in sequence. Mother's eyes spark with anger as Hazel holds a French fry with overstated daintiness, pinkie extended.

"My God, Hazel, you've eaten with us for over 40 years; what are you doing?"

"Last week, Rae Ann, you remember," the skinny woman says, all exaggerated sighs of disappointment between bites.

"Just take some dinner, Hazel and stop this, please," I say. It's important for Rick to eat and none of us needs any more aggravation.

"Since when do you care if I eat or not, Lucy?" Hazel shoots back. "Besides —" she pauses for maximum effect: "I brought something for everyone!"

I'm amazed, since no one's known Hazel to contribute anything other than dinner irritation in years. Arty stops chewing at this new development while Mother gapes. A smirky little smile sneaks over Hazel's face and her bright blue eyes sparkle, surrounded by smudges of smeared makeup, thanks to Cowboy.

Grabbing the top corners of the large bag with great importance, she empties it on top of the chicken. Dozens of Burger King's individual-serving-sized ketchup, mustard and mayonnaise packets collide with Mother's thighs and breasts, so lovingly breaded this morning. I can't believe this is happening. With a spoonful of wine-colored beets halfway to his lips, Arty stops and stares. Mother glares, her hands on her hips. Hazel meets her look. This is serious.

Rick starts sputtering and laughing, almost choking as he reaches for his coffee. But he doesn't make it to the coffee. He just chokes helplessly into the cup, trying not to spit Jell-O all over the place.

Mother's face wrinkles with concern, clearing as she sees he's okay, that he's just laughing. Her distressed look alternates between the chicken and Rick, as though she's watching a tennis match. I realize I've been holding my breath painfully in anticipation of a fight. It almost hurts to exhale.

Rick's broad shoulders heave under the robe. He pounds the table with the palms of his hands and wipes his eyes. His face is wet with laughter. Finally, he is able to speak.

I stare at him silently, again anxiously holding my breath. "Thank you, Hazel, thank you," he gasps, turning to her. "I haven't laughed like that in months."

*M*other really should stop acting like Rick is going to drop dead at any moment. He's back at work on a limited, part-time basis, and sees the doctors regularly. It's true he has to restrict his activities so he doesn't break a sweat. That might make it easier for him to catch a cold, which could put him right back in the hospital with another bout of pneumonia.

Work's good for Rick and the longer he can keep working the better, no matter how much he complains about losing his large office and finding himself reduced to performing non-stressful, low-level tasks in a tiny cubicle. The benefit of working is not the money since his stipend's only a fraction of the salary he earned as a moderately high level administrator before he got too sick to work regularly. It's that it keeps him from having to go on disability; that he sees other people when he goes to the office two or three times a week, uses his brain and walks outside at lunch time. That helps keep him involved in the world.

Not that he has any real work friends. Not since 1977, when he got that big promotion. It was a good opportunity for him but it meant leaving the small satellite office in the suburbs, his cubicle decorated with his framed drawings and the corner deli where he ate lunch every day with half the office staff, the people he'd worked with for eight years.

It was the start of commuting over three hours daily, crawling along with miles of bumper-to-bumper expressway traffic. It was the beginning of trying to find an open slot each day in the parking lot a half-mile from the Federal Building, since its monthly rates were lower than any other lot's in fourteen square blocks.

It meant entering a world where people had careers, not jobs, where co-workers competed brutally for promotions, corner offices, bigger desks, taller chairs, larger scrap pads and newer pencils. Part of him loved it, excited at the office's infighting, gloating over any move up, no matter how small. I remember how proud he was to announce he'd been assigned an office chair with arm rests.

"It may not mean much to you, but it's a real indication I could go places here. Not many get arm rests in less than six months," he said with such smugness that I wanted to laugh.

Truthfully though, not many did and as his responsibilities grew, a desk lamp, larger desk and, eventually, a private office quickly joined the chair with arm rests. He'd wound up in a prestigious corner office with two glass walls overlooking the city but complained about its chill each winter.

Ironic that he'd done so well when he'd started so humbly, at least in Matthew's eyes.

Rick was 21 and just out of college when he'd met Matthew, 14 years older and busy establishing himself as a successful young doctor in internal medicine. Though not a virgin at the time, Rick still hadn't come out with a man and had slept with only one woman, a character actress almost twice his age. They'd met during his senior year of college.

This English actress, Lily, who was from a formerly wealthy London family, worked as a part-time secretary in the university's art department and knew my brother as one of the better students there. Their casual friendship blossomed over coffee against a background of student protests, demonstrations and rallies, progressed to movie dates and peaked when Rick helped design and build the sets for an avant garde theater production she was appearing in. During the second half of his senior year he moved out of the student dorm and into her three-room apartment across town, managing to keep his actual address a secret from Mother and Arty for two months.

He'd told me about his involvement with Lily from the start and how it might not be impossible for him to love a woman after all. If I hadn't been so caught up at the time with my husband, my little girl, our first house and my own studies, I might have put more energy and interest in his direction. I was a passive bystander for the most part, only too happy to be in Toledo, Ohio, far from Mother, Arty and all family concerns at that point, but passionately interested in the student upheavals and anti-war sentiment across the country and encouraging Rick to get involved.

Apparently Rick held no secrets from Lily and she'd understood his initial reluctance and shyness, encouraging him to talk about his attractions to men, just as she had been the confidante of her own younger brother in the past. Until Lily, I'd been the only one Rick could be honest with and I'd felt an ugly, jealous churning in my stomach when he first wrote me about her.

"...Ya know, for all the rhetoric and posturing going on about a people's revolution and being free to do your own

43

thing and power to the people and all, there is little or no
tolerance, let alone acceptance, of gays here. But I trusted
her completely. The first time we went to the movies
together, I just came right out and told her I was gay.
Amazingly, all she did was nod and smile. When we talked
I felt I could say anything, be anything and it would be
okay...."

After a month or two, I began to see a new, self-confident
Rick in these letters and was able to feel happy for him, for his
sense of expectation and opportunity after graduation and his
anticipation of life's surprises.

"...I know now that any attraction to men that I feel is not
caused by any feelings of fear with women. I know now
that I can make it with a woman and make her happy. A
year ago, I couldn't have imagined writing this, living this,
but now it's true. I guess you never know who you're
going to meet around the next corner and how that will
change your life and right now I look forward to a lot (!) of
corners. I still get hard-ons for guys — more than ever, it
seems — but now it's like I wouldn't feel all scared and
virginal fucking a guy, 'cuz I know that I know how to
fuck and I have a lot (!) to offer someone. Lucy, you're
the only one who knows this...."

A time came when Mother tried to call him at the dorm,
rather than waiting for his ritual Sunday afternoon phone call
home. It didn't take her long to track down Rick's dorm
buddies and extract his current address and number.

Many phone calls back and forth followed, with Ma and
Arty yelling to me that this older woman was up to something,
trying to catch Rick and get him smoking dope and God

knows what. Depending on their moods and the particular conversation, my brother was either an innocent being led astray despite his brilliance (to hear them tell it, the brilliance they'd always praised and encouraged) or a cad taking advantage of a desperate, older woman. They were consistent, however, in maintaining that I was as much to blame as he was, setting him a terrible example by eloping with Ed, and what could they expect, with Rick looking up to me and both of us as thick as thieves, and me being such a bad influence.

Despite all of Arty's bluster, I sensed a hint of relieved pride and titillation whenever he spoke of his son "shacking up and that's what it is, shacking up — doing it with a woman old enough to be his mother!"

After I told them to stay out of Rick's business and they accused me of being an unfeeling, changeling child, everyone wished each other a variety of unspeakable tortures and deaths. After several weeks of silence, an uneasy truce was reached, along with an agreement that everyone would meet at Rick's graduation in Bloomington, Indiana. Ed was no fool and managed to get himself assigned to a two-week trip to Portland, leaving me to make the drive alone after dropping little Julie off with Ed's sister for the weekend. The university is a hot, sticky jumble of cars, caps and gowns each year as the graduates, their families and friends gather around the punch bowls filled with mysterious, pink liquids topped with white froths. Mother, Arty and I stood by the side of the refreshments table with Rick, who kept scanning the crowd for Lily. While Ma complained about the heat, her bunions and the imposition of having to meet "this older woman's people, whoever they are" and Arty stared into some indefinite middle distance, my eye was caught by a tall, dark woman in ivory crepe and pearls followed by a taller, blue-eyed male version of herself in a well-tailored navy suit.

Rick spotted her, grinned and beckoned her over. She picked her way through the crowd, kissed Rick briefly on the cheek and extended her long, elegant hand to me, saying in a cultivated voice, "Lucy, dear, so good to meet you at last. And this," she gestured gracefully with her free hand, letting her slender, coral-tipped fingers indicate the striking, sparkling-eyed man, "is my little brother, Matthew."

* * * * *

It took Rick and Matthew less than a month to move in together, much to the relief of Mother and Arty, who saw this as a sign that their son had finally come to his senses by settling in with a buddy, a roommate, until he met a girl more suitable for him. I would have been the last to tell them he already had, that he had, in fact, realized the working-class immigrant's American dream by marrying into the professional class.

Matthew loved wealth, fine crystal, fast cars and life with abandon and, because he loved my brother, I loved him, at least for a while. Although Rick's tales of their bar-crawling made me wonder if they ever slept, it was clear from the growth of Matthew's suburban medical practice and Rick's landing a modest, but steady, government job that life was falling into place for them. Though Rick was frustrated at his failure to find work in the art field, his disappointments were soothed by the convertible, trendy wardrobes and Caribbean cruises Matthew provided. Rick supplied the warmth and interior decorating, as well as ties to family with Sunday dinner and the traditional ethnic holidays at Mother's table.

Lily was living in London, part of the West End theater scene there while she supported herself by selling lingerie at Harrod's. The change was doing her good, according to Matthew and Rick, who received cheerful letters with greetings like, "Hello, you two heartbreakers" and signed, "Love to both you loves, Lily." She'd met Brian, a man her own age, a hulking floorwalker at the store who doubled as a bouncer at a local music club on weekends. They were living together and planned to marry.

Though Lily had initially seemed somewhat withdrawn and hurt at the loss of Rick to Matthew, she seemed to have forgiven all by the time they visited her and Brian two years later. I gathered it hadn't gone too well, though. Rick just flushed at my mere mention of the trip, while Matthew maintained an obstinate silence on the subject. Later, I learned from Rick that Lily kicked Brian out shortly after their visit, calling him "a faggot turncoat," and went on tour with some small Scottish drama company. She wound up teaching speech at a private school for girls in Dublin.

It was right after their return from England that Matthew's social drinking and disagreements with Rick began to take on ugly undertones and it wasn't long before Rick was calling me regularly, sometimes crying as he tried to make sense of Matthew's moods and actions.

"There's times when he's so good, just like the old Matthew, happy to be building new shelves in the garage or planting a rock garden, but when he drinks too much he gets nasty and vicious, Lucy." He paused, sniffling. "It's not just about me but about all of us in the family and how 'steel mill provincial' and limited we are and how he hates Ma's kitchen wallpaper," Rick said during one particularly painful conversation.

Dancing to the End . . . .

"He used to say he loved me, loved to be seen with me, that we looked so great together and I was his handsome young stud —" For a moment, Rick couldn't continue and when he did, his voice took on an edge and rose in pitch. "He claimed he wanted a family. Now he's ashamed of us — of me, anyway, being just a peon at HUD, and of Dad working in the mills and Lucy, he looks down on me, on all of us. I know he does and it pisses me off, dammit, it does!"

Ed's company transferred us from Toledo to Chicago, where I visited Rick and Matthew in their new home and realized Rick hadn't been exaggerating. Matthew's face was marked with lines of bitterness and anger that were quickly overshadowing these brilliant blue eyes that could still flash with exuberance. What had been a heady enthusiasm for life and sensation was deteriorating into a self-centered sarcasm that seemed to focus on my brother as Matthew directed him in serving refreshments, humiliating him for choosing the Waterford to accompany the heavy, hand-painted stoneware they'd found in Spain. Rick tried to talk about their trips or plans for the house and yard, but Matthew seemed tired and bored with most subjects, world-weary to the point of cynicism and when they talked of going out, it was no longer to the bars or shows with groups of friends, but to the bars' back rooms and men's baths for quick, anonymous sex with strangers.

"Get out of here. You don't need this," I whispered to him in the kitchen during the only visit I would ever make to Matthew's large, six-columned house in suburban Flossmoor.

"I can't," Rick said, all red-rimmed eyes and smelling of Jack Daniels. "He needs me. I take care of him and Mother brings him a hot meal at work so he eats lunch." I saw how

48

drunk my brother was, how the lines of self-pity and remorse had already started to imprint the pale flesh around his eyes and mouth. He saw my appraising look. Flushing, he said, "I drink to keep him company." After a pause when he looked away, he managed to meet my eyes again, "We had one great year like you can't imagine and I know we can get back to that. It was the best, most fulfilling year in my life. He loved me and when you've been loved by Matthew, it's like being loved by all the stars and the moon and the sky, Lucy. It's bigger than life because he can be bigger than life." He dropped his gaze. "Besides, he's all I know."

They stayed together for a total of three upwardly-mobile years, the last year in the grand Flossmoor house, saturated in bourbon and surrounded by silk sofas, hand-carved bamboo bird cages, Rick's paintings and Sarouk rugs. My brother called and talked with me nearly every day during that last six months, trying to find reasons he should stay with Matthew, too frightened to leave but miserable with Matthew's abuse and the relationship as it stood then. Ed resented these long calls especially since many came late at night or early in the morning and also because he felt my brother's life was his own problem, not mine. In time, the mention of Rick's name brought a certain tight grimness to my husband's face. I came to interpret that as his resentment and jealousy of the emotional intimacy my brother and I were once again sharing, partly because of Rick's need but also because Ed intuitively sensed — correctly — that these wrenching conversations were helping me identify problems within my own marriage.

One early spring morning when Ed and I had been separated for a couple of months, my brother finally stopped drinking; he looked at Matthew's pale flesh passed out on the bourbon-stained rug, comprehending him in a new way. Once roused to consciousness, Matthew apparently saw things differently too, since they talked seriously for hours that day. My brother hoped they would succeed in talking things out. They did. Matthew asked Rick to leave. In a week he'd moved out, leasing a small house on the Illinois-Indiana border.

Mother persisted in carrying a hot lunch over to Matthew's nearby practice for six months after the break-up. It was out of gratitude she said, since he'd cured her bunions, but who knows? She complained about them almost as much, cured or not. I think she missed his smiling presence at her kitchen table from Sundays past. She often spoke of the times when "the boys — my two boys" had helped her shampoo the carpets, wash the windows or hang the drapes.

"A second son is what he was to me, such a good friend to Rick and to all of us — I can't understand why they had such a bad fight that they can't stay friends," she said. "Even best friends have quarrels; everyone does, but that doesn't mean anything. Besides, I'm not the one fighting with him and it makes me happy to see that he eats, so I cook for him. The poor man hasn't cooked a regular meal since Rick left. And why should he? Alone like that?" But after a few months of hot lunches either Mother's bunions flared up or she finally acquiesced to Rick's wishes, because the noontime lunch deliveries ceased.

If cooking and eating hot meals at home were her measures of life's success, Rick wasn't doing too well either, since he continued to frequent men's bath houses and bars, pausing only for Sunday family dinners in Mother's kitchen and Saturday afternoons spent alternately at my house then his, where we helped each other with the yard work, often staying for suppers and aching conversations long into the night. Although Mother maintained a sporadic relationship with Matthew by calling him occasionally, within the year he moved to Hawaii as director of a substance abuse clinic in Honolulu and none of us ever heard from him again.

* * * * *

Over the years, my brother and I have had many soul-searching talks about Matthew and all the other lost loves in both our lives. Though he went on to other long-term relationships, Rick's never really gotten over Matthew. He was the one great and enduring love of my brother's life. Given the emotion he'd invested in that relationship, it's not hard to understand Rick's lingering regrets and residual bitterness. How well I know that pain when a relationship founders and disintegrates. Sometimes it's tough to remember that I'll get on with my life. Like now.

I think of Rick dancing me over to that redhead at the bar, knowing I was still hurting from the break-up with Christina and hating to see me in pain. He meant well. And certainly no one forced me to dance with Maureen, the redhead. Or talk to her. Or see her again.

He sees I'm still stuck in one of my searing, self-critical analyses of everything that's ever gone wrong in my relationships, everything that's wrong with me. Maybe that's what's causing this feeling of devastating isolation or maybe it's because I haven't really gotten over Christina yet, have never given myself the emotional time or space for coming to terms with that parting. In any case, the pain of Christina often haunts me. God knows why. I don't see her. She won't see me. At least there's no current reminders of her and I suppose I should be glad for that. She's glad, I'm sure.

Dancing to the End · · · · · · · · · · · · · · · · · ·

At least I guess she is. Who knows if I ever knew her very well, or knew her at all, for that matter? The worst days are ones like today when I wake from a sweaty dream of her. I drag myself through them unaccountably blue, missing her deeply and she seems so real to me once again — more real than the people I've seen consistently for years — more real, perhaps, than she had ever actually been.

I'm still tied to memories, physical memories, of Christina. I've got it in my head and in my gut that it's over. But not in my body. Not yet. I need to wipe away the imprint of her lips, her hands, to make myself forget what she felt like to me despite the persistence of memory.

An ex-lover of mine used to say that people can be marked by other people, that introductory or exceptional experiences, particularly physical encounters, leave their indelible stamps on us, imprinting our memory cells forever and subtly shaping our decisions and indecisions for the rest of our lives. I once scoffed at this, insisting that we're essentially free and independent beings, consciously choosing our directions. Lately I'm not so sure. Not since Christina's gone.

Finding someone new immediately after a painful break-up has never worked for me, though there's still that desire to fill in the loss at once rather than experiencing it. I should know better. I do know better. There is no filling in. That's an illusion. There is only the emptiness, probably not just for me but for most of us — and most likely forever.

Being "with some one" may help us to momentarily forget the emptiness, but sooner or later, whether or not we're with somebody, we know that void is there. We feel it inside. At first, we may blame the relationship but blame has nothing to do with what I've come to see, after all, as the human condition.

September, 1985 — LOVE THE COAT

*T*rust Aunt Alice to do the right thing. Not that we weren't concerned; we were, but with Rick's illness as the focus, other situations, not just Mother's, had to take second place.

Ma was doing the chores she's always done around the house, helping Rick if he needed it and speaking when spoken to. When she talked though, she opened her mouth and sounds came out, yet they had no real meaning for her, since she often repeated herself absently, in an empty voice.

It wasn't "I'm mad at you, so I'll give you the silent treatment," nor was it "Don't talk to me, I can't cope." Mother's malaise or burn-out or depression took the form of a drawing inward and away, so that she stared at the TV without seeing it, sat motionless at the kitchen table by herself for long periods of time and refused to answer the phone.

She used to enjoy the telephone, chatting with Hazel or Aunt Alice while she stirred the soup or scrubbed the kitchen table. Ma didn't make friends easily, but the few she had, she talked to routinely.

So we were worried about her and even though Arty was quick to wave it off, assuring us that she'd snap out of it, I saw the dark points of concern and fear in his eyes, the slight tightening of his hunched shoulders.

Dancing to the End   . . . .

"What if I suggested a therapist?" I said last Saturday afternoon after Ma's withdrawal was well into a week.

"A shrink!" Arty almost choked. "Bad enough Rick's seen one and you've been going off and on for years, but that's because you two are —"

"Say it, Arty. We're both queer."

"Stop putting words in my mouth, Lucy," he said in righteous indignation, glaring at me as he raked the grass. "That's *not* what I was going to say at all. It's just that the two of you are more sensitive, more emotional than we were in my generation. Over-emotional, if you ask me, but that's how you are. And you, Lucy, always chasing around from one thing to another — psychiatrists, meditation, Indian rituals, who knows what next! The good old Catholic church isn't good enough for you, no, you gotta go running around with a bunch of over-the-hill beatniks and hippies. If it wasn't for your mother and me, I doubt your little Julie would have been raised with any proper religion at all!"

He shook his head in disgust as Rick tried to break in, but I touched my brother's shoulder lightly, signalling him not to bother. When Arty criticized me this way, there was no way to argue. I'd learned to either walk away silently, which only fueled the fire, or let him vent. The second option got it over with faster but added to the animosity I'd felt toward my stepfather off and on for years.

I didn't respond to his attacks against what I considered to be my spiritual side. His beloved Catholicism hasn't done him much good other than giving him a poker night every Thursday with the rest of the church ushers.

My "quests," as Rick called them, have sometimes taken me to unusual and enlightening places not often visited but just as often, I've found myself in a circle of aging, tattered, self-serious pseudo-mystics in love beads singing "Michael, Row the Boat" and "Kum-Bay-Yah," trying to keep from laughing, not at them or their intentions, but at my own ill-chosen presence there. Despite the varied results of these spiritual pursuits, though, I haven't lost faith in the healing powers of prayerful meditation and group support.

Arty leaned over, tugging at a clump of brownish-gray leaves and grass wedged in the large bamboo rake. We were in the northeast part of his yard by the trellis where the purple Clematis overflows, threatening to cover the house each spring. Now the slender metal spokes of the trellis are encrusted with twisted strands of unpruned, gray, woody fiber, signalling the coming of the cold.

"Anyway," Arty said, "the way you two turned out, you certainly didn't get it from my side of the family, Rick, or Rae Ann's either, Lucy. At least our granddaughter's normal." He cleared his throat, marshalling force against his notion of the unnatural, ridding himself of any association with us. Shooting a look of accusation my way, he went on. "And there's no way therapy's going to change it — you just are. But your mother doesn't need therapy. She's exhausted from worry and needs to lean on someone, plain and simple."

He sighed, raking, leaving a 24" wide stripe of fall lawn in the carpet of grass clippings. "She doesn't lean on me because—" he broke off, staring at the leaves below. "Because — I don't know why."

I watched him, first angry at his smug arrogance, gradually becoming fascinated at an introspective, authentic Arty I'd rarely seen. Overhead the flocks of migrating Canadian geese honked their farewell messages, heard but not seen against the jet streams trailing white against the impenetrable clouds. Rick considered us from his position on the chaise lounge bordering the garden and narrowed his eyes in thought, ignoring the sketch of Julie he'd started. True to his name, Cowboy wore a western-style, red bandanna around his neck like a cattle driver. He dozed by Rick's chair, occasionally shifting in his sleep.

"Maybe if I went with Ma to therapy," I said, stubbornly hopeful. "What if I offered to just sit outside and wait for her?" I remembered how Julie, even when she was well into her teens, made sure I went with her to doctor and dentist appointments. It had helped.

Rick shook his head, wondering aloud, choosing a muted green pastel stick, replacing it with one closer to gray. "No, I don't think she'd go near anything even resembling psychiatric treatment. A priest, maybe —" He stroked Cowboy's ears and the large dog sighed.

"Your mother doesn't need a shrink; a priest, all right, but not a psychiatrist," Arty was quick to shoot back. He sighed deeply, his voice regaining its usual tone of official proclamation. "What she needs is family."

"We're her family."

"You're her daughter, Lucy. What I mean is a mother or father of her own, but they're long gone and there's just Alice." His eyes squinted and his mouth compressed at the mention of his sister-in-law's name.

Aunt Alice never liked the idea of Ma's marrying Arty less than a year after my father died in a car accident, though she knew Mother had very little money, no job skills and a small child to support. Arty needed a mother for the sensitive, artistic little boy he didn't understand and a way to make sure the laundry was done, so it was a match that made some sense, but my aunt was offended by Arty's loud voice, rough manners and refusal to take off his shoes in the house.

Alice's own husband, Charlie, had originally been one of the "chicken people," so some might wonder why she looked down on Arty. Charlie's mom and dad had run the chicken store in the middle of Poplar street. It stood there for years, mutely, without benefit of a sign or any kind of identification, since all the neighborhood people knew if you wanted a nice fresh chicken or duck, that's where you went. It survived into the 1960s, when the growth of supermarkets finally forced it out of business.

I went with my mother to the chicken store as often as I could when I was little, because there was nothing else like it, though it looked like any old, run-down house from the outside, with a rusty fence that surrounded the property. When we walked through the open doorway into the shop, the first thing to hit us was the composite smell of 100 chickens and a few dozen ducks, immediately followed by the noise of Sonny, the rooster, crowing to announce our arrival. The cackling and honking usually made it hard to hear Sonny clearly, but we knew he was there because he woke up the neighborhood each morning at 5:30 in the summertime, whenever the wind was blowing from the northeast.

My mother would pinch her nose, gagging as she moved deeper into the store's windowless gloom and inspected the birds, most of them walking around loose and pecking at the chicken feed thrown on the earth floor amid the feathers and chicken shit, some fowl seated on their nests, built on four rows of plywood planks covered with straw.

To this day, I'm not clear on my mother's criteria for a superior chicken, but after careful scrutiny, she'd point out her choice to Mr. Pagorski, the Chicken Man, and that's when he'd yell for Crazy Billy to go get it.

Dancing to the End . . . .

Billy Pagorski was born retarded, his life limited to the chicken store and the four rooms directly behind it which served as the Pagorski's home. He must have been in his late teens when I was a little kid going there with my mother. I remember him, tall and thin in his worn overalls, his dirty feet bare no matter how cold it got and the fact that he didn't talk the way the rest of us did, instead mumbling to his father, Stanley, when called, but mostly staying silent. Sometimes on my way to school, I'd pass by their place and see Crazy Billy sitting with his back against one of the rusting fence posts, gently holding two or three chickens in his lap, stroking them and muttering to them in a tender, earnest voice.

It was Billy's job to run after the chosen chicken and grab it by the neck. Sometimes this took a little while, especially if the ill-starred bird flapped out through the doorway, which was kept open all day, every day, for ventilation. The only other relief from the thick stench was the uneven humming of the large ventilator wall fan, which was clogged with decades of accumulated feathers and chicken shit and seemed to be wheezing its dying breath. Meanwhile, the commotion of Billy chasing the chicken disturbed all the remaining ducks and chickens, who fluttered wildly, making larger than usual whirlwinds of dust rise from the uneven dirt floor. If any birds tried to go through the curtained archway that separated the Chicken People's home from the store, Old Lady Pagorski, who was Mr. Pagorski's mother from Poland, jumped up from her caned chair behind the shit-stained counter and grabbed the decrepit broom she kept there for such occasions. Then this tiny Polish immigrant lady who quietly sat there every day wearing long-sleeved, high-necked dresses of an indeterminate gray-brown changed into some sort of mad chicken avenger, waving the scraggly broom at the offending animals who dared to trespass, chasing them back into the store, all the while screaming at them in what sounded like high-pitched chicken, a kind of Polish clucking.

After a short time, the chickens would revert to their usual state of mild anxiety, returning to wander casually across the counter and up onto the cash register. Old Lady Pagorski would walk slowly back to her post beneath the spotted calendar from Inland Steel, careful to drape her long skirts over her ankles and high-topped, black boots.

Usually she'd continue her conversations with the chickens, the only beings we ever saw her address, but with diminishing hostility, murmuring to them in softer and softer cackling sounds as they scratched and clucked around her, a few occasionally pecking at the tip of her boot left uncovered by the heavy, dusty dress.

By that time, Crazy Billy usually had the hapless bird by the neck and handed it wordlessly to his father, who carried the flapping creature over to the large tree trunk in the middle of the floor. There, Mr. Pagorski quickly cut off the chicken's head with a sharp hatchet and plucked the headless, quivering beast with brisk, efficient movements.

Occasionally, as Mr. Pagorski was plucking, letting the feathers float to join the others on the floor, I got to see the sight that was the high point all the neighborhood kids hoped for during a trip to the chicken store: the bird's trembling carcass jerked free from the large man's grasp and as Mr. Pagorski yelled and cursed, ineffectually trying to catch it, the dead chicken body staggered around wildly through the carpet of feathers and bird shit, spurting blood in all directions from its stump of a neck while Crazy Billy chased after it.

Once retrieved, finally plucked, and with legs and feet still attached, the chicken was unceremoniously handed over to

Dancing to the End . . . .

Mr. Pagorski's wife, Stella, a drab women in colorless dresses who wrapped the warm bird in butcher paper, rang up the sale on the encrusted cash register and wished my mother a good day with a smile as warm as the dead fowl.

I wanted to go to the Pagorskis' store whenever I knew Ma would be going, even begging her to serve chicken for dinner two or three times a week to promote these visits. Other kids in the neighborhood had found this a successful way of making regular trips to the place but Mother limited my trips there since she felt they encouraged a potentially morbid streak in me.

By the time I was big enough to go to the chicken store with my mother, Charlie, who was quite a bit older than his brother, Crazy Billy, had gone into the Army and never did return to the neighborhood business. When he was discharged after serving a number of re-enlistments, he got a job at U.S. Steel, rented a house two blocks away and married Aunt Alice a year after that. Years later, after the Pagorskis had closed the chicken store and were dead and Crazy Billy was in an asylum, the building stood empty and was listed for condemnation by the city until Uncle Charlie paid off some people at the mayor's office, bought twelve cases of beer for a series of store-cleaning parties and re-opened the place as a tavern.

Old memories linger for a long time in the neighborhood. In fact, some regular customers in Uncle Charlie's tavern swore an occasional pinfeather found its way into a Polish martini — a shot and a beer — ten years after the chicken store was just a remembrance.

So Aunt Alice lived just a couple of blocks from us when we still lived on Poplar Street, calling us over or coming by our house on the spur of the moment during the long hours the men worked at the mill. For all their insults and spats, Alice and Mother were devoted friends who enjoyed spending time together and had been allies since childhood.

The two were particularly close during Ma's eight months of widowhood, with Alice the guiding power behind all decisions. Maybe my aunt opposed Mother's marriage to Arty because she wanted to be the primary force in Mother's life, but despite Alice's domineering ways, I have always been certain of her genuine, deep and constant caring for my mother and loved my aunt for it with a protective child's unconditional devotion.

When I was an only child, I saw my mother and Aunt Alice together, helping each other, agreeing, arguing and finishing each other's sentences and I longed for a sister, for the unconscious similarities when the two simultaneously shifted in their chairs, stirred their black coffees with their left hands and moving as one, crossed their legs to the right.

After Rick and I became brother and sister, I still relished the idea of a sister since it seemed impossible to bridge the gap of gender, no matter how much life experience my brother and I shared. Though Ma often complained that Aunt Alice drove her crazy, I knew they shared a connectedness that might be unattainable for Rick and me. Mother and Alice could keep a really serious fight going for days and sometimes, weeks, but sooner or later one of them would experience a sharp twinge of recognition that they were sisters and all that it meant.

* * * * *

Yesterday, Thursday evening, I was in Mother's living room, waiting for Arty and Rick to return from the clinic, alternately writing to Julie and revising some poetry. The first poem was about daughters growing away from mothers. That subject hit me like a dead carp in the face, so I turned to the one I'd started about Maureen, a "road piece," a fantasy about the two of us happily driving across America, but the tension of the wait distracted me from my work. It's the waiting in between that's an indefinite Hell separating tiny upsurges of hope from the longer stretches of day-to-day medication schedules, blood tests, eye checks and the dangerous, slippery slopes of dread that lead down into despair. There are waits to hear the results of Rick's most recent lab tests, treatments and side effects; the wait for news of a possible slot in the waiting list for a California clinic reportedly extending the life of AIDS patients by as much as three years; waits for news about experimental drugs being scrutinized by the FDA. It's not good for Mother to fret alone, especially with her weak heart, so yesterday I drove directly from work to wait with her for the latest blood work results. They can make the difference between Rick remaining home or returning to the hospital. They can signal another stabilization or a dip that could start that steep, final descent.

Though I didn't really mind waiting with Mother, in the last year I've often resented the amount of time I've had to spend over here with the family, the most time since leaving for college 19 years ago. That's certainly got nothing to do with the way Rick and I get along, since we've always been close, often choosing each other's company over the friendship of others. It's the stress I feel around Mother and Arty, the tension between them and around them that they seem to spontaneously generate that so often makes me want to avoid them. If it hadn't been for Rick's illness, I would never have been spending so much time with them again.

Although we'd just had her homemade stuffed peppers
for dinner, Ma was making a grilled cheese sandwich,
watching the buttered bread browning in the pan.

"Don't you want anything? A sandwich?" She always
asks although she knows I'll fix myself something if I'm
hungry.

"Not really. Maybe later."

"You don't have to ask, you know," she said, furrowing
her brow and wiping her hands on the old apron she wore. "I
worry because sometimes you forget to eat."

I know. My mother has never forgotten to eat in her life,
not even during labor pains. In fact, Mother delights in telling
and retelling the tale of her 24-hour labor with me, when she
postponed going to the hospital as long as possible.

She had been awakened by the first strong contraction, so
had paced and read the newspapers for three hours. My dad
— my real father, not Arty — was at the steel mill, working
double shifts and she hadn't wanted to bother him until she
was certain the baby was about to be born. So she'd paced
some more, then prepared and ate a large meat loaf dinner.

As each carefully-diced onion had been evenly browned
with the fresh parsley in sputtering butter, she'd alternately
moaned and hummed, softly at first, but louder as she'd
peeled the potatoes and watched them boil.

The way Mother continues the story, by the time she was
plunging the masher into the aluminum pan of boiled
potatoes, "I didn't know if I was even going to get to eat,
honest to God. The pains were still four minutes apart, but
who could know with a first baby? So I looked at that nice,
brown meat loaf with my lovely, fluffy mashed potatoes and
the cute little carrot slices I'd cut with a crinkle cutter, so

darling, and knew it would have been a sin — a sin not to eat such a dinner! So I ate."

After that, according to her retelling, she'd sat by the kitchen table, gripping its edges with every contraction, waiting alone with only the meat loaf for consolation, glad that she'd thought to keep up her strength.

Mother is always careful to remind me or any other listener to this birth saga that between contractions, she'd gotten up and neatly stored the leftovers in covered dishes, "so your father would know I'd made his supper for him. No matter what, I always made my man's supper." I have the feeling she remains convinced that more thorough attention to food preparation and storage on my part would have salvaged my marriage to Ed. Maybe she's right.

Whenever I hear this story of Mother's heroic labor and how she'd managed to do the dishes and put them away, I can't resist the temptation to ask her why she hadn't scrubbed and waxed the kitchen floor, cleaned out the cupboards and washed down the walls while she was at it.

Usually she glares and lectures on the value of responsibility or, occasionally, just settles for a sharp look followed by a martyred, "Never mind. I'm just saying. You were no easy child to have, you know, and you weren't any better to raise. Good thing I ate before I went to the hospital. They never feed you there and when they do, it's no good anyway. Everything's cold. Just like the chicken and mashed potatoes at Jack Gorski's funeral lunch. Everything was cold. God only knows how long it had been sitting out in the platters and you'd think Fran Gorski would have sent the food back to be re-heated, but no, she didn't. She just expected us all to eat it the way it was, so what could we do? We ate it. But it gave me gas."

So gas is the final, perhaps most lasting, impression left by the late Mr. Gorski, known to the children of the neighborhood as a good-hearted man, always ready to give us pieces of penny candy from those large, round, glass canisters on his newspaper counter, even if we didn't always have the pennies or it was much too close to our supper times. Of course, the sugar dulled our appetites for those chicken dinners with sauerkraut, rye bread and creamed corn and our mothers ranted about children rotting their teeth and growing up stunted from a lack of proper food and vitamins, the direct and inevitable result of eating penny candy right before dinner time.

On those few days when we'd managed to sneak into Gorski's store without being caught and stopped by someone's mother, Ma felt deeply and sincerely wounded by Mr. Gorski's actions, as though he'd singled her out to suffer over the thousands of pounds of potatoes she'd peeled for us, all those glazed carrot coins, painstakingly sliced from carrots carefully chosen for their uniform diameter, with only our childish ingratitude as payment for her efforts.

*   *   *   *   *

Mother was standing by the stove with spatula in hand, watching her sandwich reach the proper stage of golden brown perfection that only the best grilled cheese sandwiches achieve when the phone rang last night.

"Aren't you going to get that, Ma?" No answer. "You want me to get it?"

"No." A flat, definitive answer.

"Why not? You're not getting it."

"I know," she answered in a tight voice.

"So I'll get it," I insisted, feeling irritated.

"No," she said in that flat, brick-wall stubborn tone that makes me raise my voice.

"Pick it up, for God's sake!" The phone must have been on its fifth or sixth ring.

"Well, all right," she finally said, her voice filled with suffering and reproach at such an unreasonably demanding daughter.

It was Aunt Alice and Ma was blue and nervous, so I expected a fair amount of complaining from my mother's side of the conversation, but was unprepared for the eruption.

On and on she went, focusing her helplessness and anxieties on the cost of doctors and treatments, the high prices for prescriptions, even the little things like gas for the trips back and forth and three new pairs of pajamas for Rick.

Mother never made any direct reference to the sweats or spells of coughing and weakness that drained my brother or of the Niagara nosebleeds or the proliferation of Kaposi's Sarcoma spots. Instead, her approach to the situation, to any difficult situation, concentrated on its cost in dollars, a measurable, tangible drain easily understood and deserving of sympathy, socially acceptable if the villains involved were associated with professions and institutions at best suspect. Doctors and hospitals were perfect.

Up until then, Ma had confined her concerns to me and Arty, sharing only occasional, off-hand details about the costs with her sister, but a year of increasing frustration with rising medical expenses and diminishing optimism exploded last night onto Aunt Alice.

Ma ranted at her sister against the endless medical fees, the specialists who conferred, conferred, conferred, decided nothing, then quickly sent their bills and the equally galling slowness with which the insurance company mailed reimbursement checks, frequently omitting the cost of any treatment deemed "experimental."

"This whole damn thing is experimental, for God's sake, Alice," she said, rising from the kitchen chair and raising her voice from the dead level that had distinguished it for over a week. "He's the first diagnosed case in all of Northwest Indiana and nobody even knows how this virus works, let alone how to treat it. This thing's only been around for what — three or four years — so they try this, they try that, they do another IV and another and there's no veins left after awhile, so they try something else. But the insurance people say these aren't usual expenses, so they don't pay. Or they only pay a small part and that's after months of hassling." She had turned off the flame under her sandwich and was pacing with the phone cord wrapped around her then, treading a short, narrow path from the wall phone to the sink and back, opening and closing drawers, re-folding dish towels and stacking pot holders.

After a lengthy silence on Ma's end of the conversation, she said, "Well, Alice, I've got to go now. Lucy's here and we're going to go to the store pretty soon, whenever the fellows get back. I can't stand going food shopping alone any more. Everything costs so much. It just takes everything out of me. I'll call you soon, I promise." She abruptly replaced the receiver but didn't touch the sandwich.

I've learned to let her be when she's upset, so I finished the letter in silence and turned again to the poetry, stopping only when a persistent ringing pulled me from my work. "Ma?" I called. "Do you want me to get the door? Will you?"

We got there at the same time, opening the door together to the sight of Aunt Alice, stunning in a mauve suit, pearls

67

and pumps and brilliant red hair billowing in the wind, the tips shining golden in the porch light. For a moment, the sight of that hair, radiant in the deep yellow light, reminded me of Maureen and her red hair, though hers is more gold with reddish highlights and she comes by it naturally. Cowboy silently joined us, watchful and waiting.

Aunt Alice's arms were straining with the effort of holding two bulging paper bags of groceries. Her face, usually so pretty with its high, fine cheekbones and perfect makeup, was working furiously as she looked at us, weeping. The quiet of the front porch was torn by the force of Aunt Alice's cry, a wail that rose from her crooked arthritic toes into her Achilles' tendons, ran up her knees, thighs, groin, belly and into her spine and neck to exit from her open, twisted mouth. Cowboy yelped, a high, sharp bark recalling his wolf ancestry.

"You're my baby sister," Aunt Alice cried. "I can't stand to see you living like this. God, Rae Ann, why didn't you tell me it had gotten to this point? Was it pride? I had no idea you had it so hard. How could you not tell me 'til now? Me, your own sister, and you don't come to me? Here — some food and a coat. Take it." The tears poured out with renewed volume. "Jesus, Rae Ann. Jesus, Jesus Christ. I never thought I'd live to see the day I'd be happy poor Momma was dead. But today," she said, pausing to snuffle in breath, "today, I'm glad she's not here to see this!"

Mother gaped unbelievingly. Alice thrust one of the bags at her, freeing a hand to grope for a tissue in her purse. I stepped toward my aunt, taking the other sack.

"Lucy, get that stuff into the freezer right away," she said. "There's a couple of beef roasts, a small turkey and some steaks in that one. Took them from my own freezer." She paused to blow her nose loudly, twice, and spoke to my mother. "There's canned vegetables, noodles, rice, a big can of coffee and a canned ham in that other bag, Rae, and you're going to love the coat. Believe me, it's a perfect light weight fall coat, just right for this time of year. It's like new, worn only twice."

"Aunt Alice—" I started, but Mother cut in, saying, "Alice, for God's sakes, what is this? Get in the house."

"Yes, you're right, of course. We don't want people to know," Alice said, walking in quickly. Mother and I followed with the groceries, accompanied by the watchful Cowboy.

"Know what, Alice? What are you talking about?" Mother insisted, setting her sack down next to the stairs. I put mine down next to it.

Aunt Alice sniffed loudly, slamming the heavy oak door shut and taking a deep breath before focusing her red-rimmed eyes on Mother. "If only you had said something before. After all, Rae Ann, we're family and that's what family is for. We're here to do for each other, for God's sake. Why you let some kind of false pride keep you from telling your own sister —"

"Tell you *what?*" Mother practically screamed.

Aunt Alice fell silent for a moment, glancing down briefly, looking up. "The money problem, Rae Ann. I had some idea what you'd been going through, but you should have told me things were so hard. You should have trusted me. These groceries will help tide you over and here, a nice coat, Rae Ann. Take it."

"A coat?" Disbelief reverberated off the walls of the entrance hall.

"A raincoat. Really, it's a very nice coat. And Rae, it's got the loveliest lining that zips right out so you can wear it all year 'round." Alice sniffled again. "It's like new, believe me."

"Alice, what do you mean? We have food. We have clothes. The insurance will come, sooner or later. It just takes time, that's all," Mother said. She took her sister's hands in both of her own. "I was only just talking, 'cause who can I talk to?"

They looked down at the bulging sacks, catching each other's eyes, laughing.

"Go on, try it on," Alice says, opening the coat. "You see, a zip-out lining! It's a very nice coat. Worn only once, like I said."

Mother hugged her, looking better than she had for weeks with her sister's arms around her. I put the groceries away and heard Cowboy's welcoming barks and yips of joy at the sound of Rick's car pulling into the driveway.

October, 1985 — I TOUCHED YOU

*T*oday it happened. Today I stopped hating them. This morning I sat in my therapist's office, that office in the red brick building in the city of Chicago, the same office I have sat in each Friday for over two years straight. I hated my hands on Fridays; I had hated them for over two years. Every Friday, no matter how anguished or relaxed, no matter how frightened or seemingly at ease — each Friday I had sat in that chair and faced that therapist and hated those icy-cold, sweaty-blue hands.

After the first year in therapy had passed, I had come to see those wet, twitchy hands as a symbol of an anxiety I couldn't beat. I'd kept reassuring myself to be patient, to relax, to give it time, that sooner or later it would happen.

Sure it would.

Sooner or later, I would become more at ease with her, this therapist, this person I'd spilled my guts to. Yes, that's it. She's a real person, a person named Lynn.

Maybe the first thing you might notice about her is her right arm. She doesn't have a hand there. She was born that way. You might admire her long, pretty, blonde hair, all tied back and hanging down. Lynn's a little woman: small bones, small frame and a small, delicate face. And just one hand.

Such a contrast to me, with my dark curly hair falling messily all over my eyes, my nervous twitching as I check my slacks for non-existent lint, my incessant smoking.

She lacks one hand. What do I lack?

All I know is that I've always felt like something was missing in me, that I wasn't truly a real person but some kind of cardboard impersonation instead; that no matter what I did, it would never be enough — that I could never be enough, would never be whole.

Yes, this was Lynn, a real person, a person I wanted to relax with, to be myself, to be at ease. And it wasn't happening.

But sure, it would happen. Sure, sure. And someday, along with having warm, dry hands, I'd stop being so scared of others, so scared of myself. That's right; it was just going to happen.

Just a matter of time.

But it never did. I had stopped thinking it ever could. I had stopped thinking of even talking about those damned hands with her because that threatened me so much. I had never spoken about them to her, to my therapist, to that person I'd risked so much with. It meant that much to me.

It was bad enough that I knew what a scared wreck I felt like so much of the time. That was enough, being the most terrified person I knew, had ever known, for that matter, no matter how many others found me competent and coping. But it was too much for me to speak about the outward signs of this internal struggle since I've grown enough to realize the issue at hand is usually a lot bigger than the symptoms. Sometimes I used to talk out loud, used to curse myself while I was driving back home in my car.

You coward. You idiot. What is wrong with you? Over two years in therapy and you can't even relax enough about yourself to stop having sweaty palms, to stop feeling like a dead salmon? What are you, a person, a real person, a warm, warm-blooded mammal or a dead fish?

"You want so much change and you want to do it so quickly. You should be less hard on yourself," Lynn would say, usually pausing for a long, appraising breath. "You've always expected too much of yourself. Change requires patience. It doesn't occur overnight."

Okay, not overnight, but it's not overnight; it's two years, more than that, do you see, do you understand? Two years, and I'm feeling better, I know myself more, I understand my needs, my divorce, my former husband, sometimes even my daughter as a result, but, my God! Two years straight without so much as a single missed therapy session and still this sweaty palm crap! When will it end? Is it ever going to end? It's not going to end.

Jesus, Maureen and I joke about it, but I'm still the sweaty palm kid when we hold hands, not all the time but occasionally, and it upsets me. It embarrasses me. She laughs about it, says she still gets nervous sometimes around me and gets clammy hands too, no matter how intimate we've been, but it doesn't seem to bother her the way it does me. Funny that I don't see nervously wet palms as a liability in anyone else, but I surely do in myself. From the time I first became old enough to comprehend my own inclination toward fine-boned beauty, I've had a general dislike for my body and my hands in particular, with their short, blunt fingers.

Maureen has lovely hands, slender and long-fingered, tapering to delicate wrists. I think of them at work in the spare bedroom she's converted to her darkroom, laboriously manipulating light and time and chemical reactions to produce the solarized special effects in her photographs. I think of the sense of mystery and magic Maureen says she feels when the paper in the developing tray slowly surrenders its image, sensing it as somehow different from the emotion I bring to my writing, pounded out on the keyboard with thick fingers and a fine mind attempting to create elegantly crafted word pictures.

Maureen carefully, gracefully, hangs the dripping wet prints from the line strung in the darkroom with only the plopping of the drops on the newspaper-covered carpeting forming the music she works by. She says she needs no other. That, and her hope for professional recognition as a fine art photographer suffice to keep her laboring at the advertising assignments that support her.

There's a slim-boned elegance to Maureen's hands whether she's working in her darkroom, washing dishes, framing her photos or feeding peanuts to Ralph, her macaw. Sometimes the bird rides on her shoulder, whistling and speaking to her in his low, parrot-y baritone as she moves gracefully throughout the apartment crammed with her books, portfolios and family photos. When she gives him a treat like fresh broccoli or sliced apple, she talks in a chatty, mothering tone to him like a child, telling him he is *such* a good bird, then gently feeds him tidbits with her long, slender fingers. I have been known to fall in love with people because of their shapely hands and delicately defined wrists.

Rarely do I ever have a sense of anything in myself that might stir another so, and I get pissed off at my chronic self-doubt and low self-esteem, my frustratingly slow progress in therapy despite years of weekly sessions and daily meditation.

"How do you feel today," Lynn asks me, neither smiling nor frowning, but shifting slightly in her chair to reach her steaming mug of coffee. "I sense a lot of tension in you."

A lot of tension? "I feel like I'm standing in the middle of this shit pile, a giant mound of it, all around me. I feel like I'm digging myself out of it, digging myself out of this huge mountain, but all I have is this tiny little shovel. And I'm tired, God damn it, I'm tired! It's been two solid years and I'm sick and tired of digging at this same old shit!"

"It's been there a long time." She sits quietly centered in her high-backed, upholstered arm chair.

My God, will it ever end? Please God, let it end! Haven't I worked hard, God, haven't I tried, even when it hurt? And I was a good kid, God, I kept on going. But I'm not a kid. I'm well past thirty. And I'm not in some basketball game, I'm somewhere else. If only I knew where.

"You've said you sometimes feel fragmented, disconnected. That's a big risk to admit that. Give yourself some credit."

Fragmented isn't the word, isn't close, for God's sake! I can't begin to describe feeling like I'm here, there, all over, running, still running, running into myself, colliding, shattering. And there isn't even a single me to collide with! I am a series of floating pieces, a string of large blobs. And now, my God, I can't find it, God, help me please, I can't find my left leg! I lost it somewhere, somewhere in this strange cloudy place I'm floating in. God knows where. Now I can't find me. Lost that somewhere, too.

"I imagine that fragmented feeling must be one of the most frightening things you experience."

The fall rain slants against the window, splattering with small explosions at each impact, creating the only sounds in the tiny office. Lynn sits, still and serene, while I have lost my direction, my surroundings. I have lost my limbs, I have lost my senses. My God, I have lost my senses! I am out of my senses. I am a freako gone bananas on a shit pile and please help, please, please help, because I need help and don't know the way, I lost the way, can't find the way out.

"Can we talk more about this feeling of fragmentation? As you begin to understand it, you'll become less afraid," she says quietly, seemingly removed from anything like fear.

Talk, talk, talk, talk, talk. All this talk and I still can't get out. Keep on working, try to keep going, try to remember. I can do it. It hurts but I have to go back. But if I go back, where am I now? Can I ever come back to it? I'm afraid to go in. I want to come back someday. At least I think I do and I'm afraid I'll never make it back. I'm terrified, but I'm going. I'm letting go. It's gone too far to stop it. I started it and I have to go in now.

* * * * *

Two years of weekly sessions, concentrated effort and now what? Change. Yes, change, so fast, sometimes almost too fast, but not so fast I'm not still standing.

Confidence, fear. Coping, headaches. Independence, loneliness. **I'M STILL STANDING.**

Contentment, hives. Risks, stomach-aches. **I'M STILL STANDING.**

Accomplishment, self-doubt. Self-reliance, Rolaids. **I'M STILL STANDING.**

* * * * *

One day, it was like a dream; I can't express it, really. One day, my throat was all achy and sore from too many cigarettes and I put down the one I was smoking. Who knows what I was thinking or what got into me? Lynn was talking about the importance of small steps in growth, however frustratingly insignificant they might seem, and I wanted to interrupt. But I didn't. I reached out to her and I touched her, touched her one hand. I had never touched her before. I couldn't believe I had touched her. I raised my head to look at her, to see if it was all right, and I saw that Lynn was looking at me, staring. I thought I might cry.

She gazed steadily at me and she was so moved, so surprised, amazed. It was like she was in shock when she said, "You touched me."

I looked at her eyes and it reminded me of seeing the eye of a camera opening to let in the light, only slowly, very slowly. I could see the center of her eyes, opening slightly, bit by bit and I could gradually see deeper inside until I felt we'd merged, had fused into a single force.

I stared into her eyes; I stared at me through her, as if I were in a dream and waking up.

She repeated it and this time it was as though it was a voice inside me: "You touched me."

I heard myself say, "Lynn — I touched you. Alive! My God, I feel so alive!"

She smiled, saying, "I'm glad. I suspected it all the time." We howled with laughter until we wept. It was such a crazy thing to say.

She'd known I was alive all the time. And at that moment, I knew it.

* * * * *

77

The minutes and the hours and the days became weeks and months. And again, I became scared and lost and lonely, sometimes worse than ever; I wondered if it had, in fact, been a dream. I was afraid to ask her. And the minutes and the days and the weeks rolled into a hard, gray lump inside me and I knew I had to rest, had to relax. No matter how much they were needed, the moments of genuine respite were fleeting and infrequent.

*   *   *   *   *

And today it happened. I didn't even realize it at first. I was just sitting, smoking, playing with a loose wooden button on my tweed blazer while I listened to her talk about my growth and fears. Then I felt it, felt them, felt those damn, wonderful hands. They were warm and dry and attached to these arms and were a part of me.

And they were okay. Really okay. As a matter of fact, they were fine, they were perfectly fine and they were a part of me. So I shouted at her, interrupted her in the middle of her sentence.

"Hey! Take my hand! Look, feel it. It's warm and dry and not all icy and clammy the way it used it be. Feel it, squeeze it, squeeze it, hard! I used to hate the way they'd clam up in here and I could never even talk to you about it. I was ashamed, so ashamed. But look — it's okay now. It's okay."

*R*ick and I are having troubles. He's so angry about my having a job, a new relationship, some kind of a productive, creative life outside of blood tests and sickrooms. He just freezes up or changes the subject with me whenever I mention these outside aspects of my life but denies any resentment. I loathe feeling I must keep important parts of my life unspoken, hidden, especially from him and especially in a life where so many essentials had been secret for so long.

I hate to say it but I think he's just plain jealous. His so-called friends, once so numerous and eager to crowd his large weekend house parties, have been equally quick to desert him. He no longer has a job to go to, not even part-time, nor lovers. That's unbelievably hard on him but I won't put the brakes on this relationship with Maureen just because it's coming along at a bad time for him.

Since I came out, there were times he was knee-deep in men while I was painfully healing from broken relationships, desperately getting up the nerve to go to a women's coffee house or concert alone. There were times I had no job, envying his security in a government post, and the nights I felt isolated, lonely, loveless. I can understand his resentment. I have a memory and know how it feels to hear other people's phones ringing when it seems yours never will again.

As it is, I spend too much time feeling preoccupied and divided, often worrying about Rick when I'm at work or with Maureen and never having enough time. More and more since my brother's diagnosis a year ago in 1984, Mother and Rick want me to come by after work once or twice a week; then, too, the family Sunday dinner and afternoon visit seem to be command performances, except for the times Rick's hospitalized. Sunday's the only full day I don't work and as Julie's grown older, more involved in her own life, her frequent absences from the weekly family dinner seem to necessitate my routine presence to keep the peace.

For the last few months, Rick's seemed relieved I've stopped brooding over Christina — after all, it was Rick who had virtually introduced me to Maureen, dancing me over to her in that bar four months ago. But since I've started spending larger amounts of time with her regularly this fall, his attitude toward Maureen has changed.

"Don't go getting serious. Why would you want to go and do that," he said last weekend, sketching my portrait in pastels. "You've got your freedom, your work, your friends, your daughter, even if we don't hear from her — a good life, and that's nothing to take for granted. Hold still."

"I don't take it for granted. Why would you think I do?" I answered, looking straight at him in surprise.

"So appreciate it, enjoy it. Why can't you just date her on a casual basis?" He challenged with every word.

"Besides," he said, looking down to the drawing, "you'd have serious differences to work out. She's not from some little mill town, like we are. She's from a wealthy family of professionals — her father and grandfather are doctors in Winnetka, for God's sake, and her mother drives a sports car!" He snorted in frustration. "We're from working class, immigrant stock. Our grandparents came over here from Poland with less than a dozen words of English, total, and a few bundles of clothes. We may have graduated from college and bought nice homes in better neighborhoods than we grew up in, but that doesn't change where we came from."

We were speaking in the large, white bedroom that was his until he grew up and left this house, the big old house we moved to four blocks east of Poplar Street shortly after my mother married Arty. For years after my brother had moved out, Mother used it as a sewing room. It's become Rick's room again, the walls hung with his paintings and the charcoal drawings he's recently done tacked up on any available space. He looked around at his childhood room, perhaps comparing it unfavorably with the opulently Oriental bedchamber he'd created for himself in the eight-room home he'd owned for six years. He'd been forced to sell that house less than a year ago.

He paused for breath: "Money and class are just part of it. This family can be nuts and we're not like other people, you and I, and never have been. That alone's plenty to make us different, even from people in the neighborhood, let alone from a good north side family. And crazy or not, wealthy people are loony in a classier way." He flung the hair from his eyes with an angry, frustrated hand.

I said nothing, knowing that this good family, according to Maureen, has an emotionally distant grandfather and a father who can be charming but is prone to outbreaks of violent rage, bullying all around him into submission. Her alcoholic sister's a surgeon married to a workaholic, verbally abusive CPA and her ineffectual mother is a chain smoker alternately devoted to keeping the peace and getting out of the house as much as possible.

Yet it's undeniably true that my family would look odd or old-fashioned, perhaps even ignorant to outsiders, and I know there's an blue-collar part of them I'm not really proud of and would rather leave behind. I hate myself for my snobbery and insecurities, but with the exception of Rick and Julie, I don't like introducing my family to any of my friends or associates, many of them artists or poets, like myself.

Last week, Maureen had finally convinced me to go with her to her parents' large, red brick Winnetka home and I ultimately went as much out of curiosity as anything else. Though so straight forward much of the time, I sense odd, fleeting moments when something triggers Maureen and she clouds over, her talk drifting off into tangents seemingly calculated to leave vague, insubstantial impressions of her life guarded by impenetrable barriers. Or it could simply be my need to see her as an intriguing mystery since we come from such different sides of the tracks. In any case, curiosity overcame my reluctance to meet this couple who lived, literally, high on a hill.

When we'd visited last week, Maureen had parked her Nissan Sentra we'd washed for the occasion between the shining Lincoln Town Car and Porsche in the circular driveway. The front porch was adorned with wreaths of interwoven branches, hay stacks with piles of gourds between them and Halloween jack-o-lanterns for the season, decor that would have been stolen or smashed on Mother's porch. The Winnetka pumpkins flickered serenely with real candles. That evening, Steven, her father, had grilled thick steaks on the oversized outdoor gas grill, laughing at the meal's informality since their maid wasn't working that night, but had at least done the side dishes and set the table before leaving. Pat, her mother, had made a point of showing me her new silver sports car and I'd wondered what it was like to have such expensive toys.

At one point in the evening, Maureen pulled me over in one of the many dark, carpeted hallways in that big house, hugging me tightly, wrinkling my linen blouse and after a swift furtive look, kissing me hotly on the mouth.

"See," she'd said, pressing herself tightly to me, "tonight isn't so bad, is it? We're just average people, a family like anyone else."

"Look," Rick said, his voice a knife cutting into my thoughts, "Wealth and class are power. No amount of your poetry or artistic visions or my paintings, for that matter, can minimize that. Neither of us fit in with money, no matter how much art and culture we've absorbed. He leaned back in his chair, narrowing his eyes. "Face it; that's out of our league."

I felt like I'd been struck, whether by the force of his anger or the truth of his words I couldn't say. Cowboy, who'd been lying asleep between us on the braided rug, stirred to consciousness with a low, moaning sound deep in his throat. Seeing my hurt, Rick softened his tone, sketching broad strokes of pastel chalk to suggest my cable knit sweater. "You've been a serious creative writer for some time, Lucy, scrimping and saving for workshops and seminars. It's not like you're some rich man's indulged daughter playing at poetry. You've sacrificed." His hand flew on the sketch.

His voice grew harsh again. "Your girlfriend may be living the bohemian life of a photographer in Hyde Park for awhile, but both her grandfather and father come from money, she comes from money and eventually, she'll go back to it because money always goes to money. You'll see."

I silently admitted to myself that I've seen the signs of precisely such potential trouble — or rather, have felt them as insecurities brewing inside me, small rumblings of discomfort in the face of Maureen's easy assumption of status, education and privilege, her expensively furnished apartment decorated with Oriental rugs and signed original photographs by Eugene Atget, Imogen Cunningham and Man Ray.

Recently, she'd told me the story of her first lesbian heartbreak: years ago in California, she'd come home early, surprising Victoria, her college lover, in bed — their bed — with Ted, her best friend from Graphic Design class. She'd dashed out of their apartment, checking into a large downtown hotel "to think things over in a Jacuzzi," she'd told me. I had been dumbfounded, not at the scenario of betrayal, but at her casual ability to afford a Los Angeles hotel room with a whirlpool bath on a college student's budget and even more, at her natural certainty that this was the customary course of action to have taken, unquestioned in any way.

Such a contrast to my broken heart that final, bitter night years ago when I'd slammed out the door leaving Sharon, my first serious woman lover. Although I was through graduate school and working at a small Chicago paper at the time, there were large school loans to pay off and money was always tight. Rick was away on business so I'd spent that night in an all-night donut shop, channeling my pain into poetry and parceling out change for coffee refills, returning home with $1.16 in my pockets. The poems had eventually appeared in a small literary journal, which paid me the princely sum of two free copies for my work. There's a book shelf at home that's jammed with two copies of many different literary magazines, the sum total of my compensation for five years of poetry, plus my memories of the two gas bills and a phone bill I paid with that check from *The New Yorker,* the only real money I've ever received for my poems. Intellectually I know that track record is better than average but deep inside I still feel like a failing, starving artist. No matter how materially successful I might ever become, having money will never feel natural to me, let alone assumed or assured. In a way that's helped me, given me an edge and made me stay hungry.

"What am I supposed to do, Rick? Stop seeing Maureen just because she comes from money and I've had to squeak through life scrimping and saving?"

"Wait. Just wait and see," he said, flipping the hair from his eyes with irritation.

"Stick to our own kind, whatever that is? Someone with a foot in both worlds, but not right for either? Or give up poetry or any professional writing for that matter, since there's no money in it?" Sometimes I get so impatient with Rick; it showed then, though I didn't want it to.

"You just want to nail down the relationship," he said with a smug complacency.

"What exactly do you mean by that?"

"You think by formalizing the relationship with some kind of a commitment that it'll last forever. That's what you want, no matter how you deny it. It's what you miss. But if you two split, it's just as messy, commitment or not." He spoke with the finality of a judge pronouncing sentence.

I thought about this, analyzing and balancing my shifting need for security against the heady joy of living a single, unattached life, that feeling of freedom, of splendid isolation as I unlock the door and walk into my living room filled with things I alone have paid for and knowing the only emotional eggs I have to walk on are my own.

"I don't know. It's scary — being in a relationship and not being in one."

He gave me a grunt from deep in his throat. "You just don't want to be dumped. Who does? But nothing stops the chances of it happening."

"No, of course it doesn't." I remembered Matthew and the time he lived the high life of conspicuous consumption with my brother. The familiar look on Rick's face told me he was remembering too, recalling the initial closeness the two had shared, reliving and grieving that archetypal loss as he has ever since. "But you're right. I don't want to be dumped, of course not. I'm feeling ready to shatter. Right now, I don't think I could take it."

"Sure you could, Sis. We both have and the only thing we are now is older, stronger and wiser. So there!" he concluded, grinning broadly. "Besides," he said, his tone going hoarse and dark, "It's not like I'm going to be around that much longer; maybe six months with luck. If you two have anything worth working on, it will keep. Just wait 'til I'm gone." That was it, just like that, in a matter-of-fact tone, his face set and hard. He stood, tall and straight, setting his pastels and sketch pad on the desk.

"Jesus, Rick!"

"Jesus has nothing to with it," he said. "I just want to know you'll be here for me when I need you." He turned and left the room, Cowboy following silently at his heels.

* * * * *

I let several days pass; when I drop by to visit him this evening, he is alone in his room sitting by the dresser, wearing a brand new baseball jacket half zipped over a dark T-shirt. He's preening, shifting in the chair to catch the subtle nuances he seeks in the mirror's three-way reflections.

He likes to look good and always has. Before he got sick, my brother had spent 10 years working out in health clubs and could bench-press 320 pounds. At 6'1" and 190 pounds, he was one gorgeous guy. He weighs 165 now.

"Come here. Look at this jacket."

"Nice, Rick. Very nice. Where'd you get it?"

"My father. Said he saw it in a window display at Carson's and thought I'd like it. And get this." He looks at me squarely in the face, his eyes bright with happiness. "It wasn't even on sale. It's part of this season's designer collection and he bought it for me just because he thought I'd like it, paid full price and everything."

"That's great," I say and it is, a burgundy red creation in corduroy, its sporty lines set off with navy trim, ribbed collar and cuffs.

That color combination reminds me of the red and blue saddle shoes I bought when I was 23. They were suede, with bright red laces, clunky things that were dancey and lighthearted despite their bulk. Anyway, I had to have them and I don't remember what they cost, but we all spent money on clothes then, funny clothes in bright colors.

The first day I'd worn those crazy red and blue suede shoes I'd been married. My husband Ed, all commuter executive in his dark suit and white shirt, took one look at them, shook his head and said, "No. You're not really going to wear those, are you? Not outside the house? Not with me! Not even to drop me off at the train. Don't you dare embarrass me that way. Don't you know you're my wife?"

Even if I hadn't been sure before, I'd resolved on the spot to wear them as much as possible, especially around Ed and started planning a bohemian-chic wardrobe around blue and red shoes with red shoelaces.

Dancing to the End . . . .

They remained good-looking for years. I was taught to take good care of things so I was a sound maintainer of seemingly everything except relationships. Years ago a portrait painter I'd interviewed told me a well-maintained, high quality, hand made brush would outlive three human life spans. If true, it's not a bad thought to keep in mind.

Those blue shoes were amazingly sturdy too, now that I think about it. I started wearing them when I went back to school to finish my undergraduate degree in English at the University of Chicago. Despite their associations with unrequited love, broken vows and a broken marriage, I'd kept the shoes through graduate school, when I'd first become an active member of Chicago's lesbian community, and wound up relegating them, at last, to the ranks of old clothes worn only for yard work or camping trips. That was during the first time I'd lived with a woman, had just gotten my first job and with it, my first career wardrobe of skirted suits and blazers. Actually, those blue suede shoes had outlasted quite a few of the jobs and women in my life.

But it was Susan, a women from that past era in my life who'd made the phone call a year ago. The agonizing fear of the diagnosis I'd dreaded had made the wait for that particular call seem like years. Each morning for almost a week it had been that fear awakening me, not the clock radio, and I'd forced myself through another day of not knowing.

Susan had run the hospital lab and I'd begged her to tell me Rick's test results the minute she had them from the Center for Disease Control. After her initial refusal she'd relented and called, perhaps out of pity or maybe for old time's sake, catching me just as I was leaving the house to direct the dress rehearsal of a comedy. I'd been active in community theater for years prior to Rick's illness.

"I guess it really is," she'd said, her voice low and serious.
"You guess or you're sure, Susan? Dr. Mitchell's sure?"
"Yeah, he is. Sure. CDC confirmed the diagnosis. I'm
sorry, Lucy. I know you're close to your brother."
Heat and cold had waved over my head, down my torso
and legs in alternating masses of flame and chill. I'd found
myself rocking back and forth slightly, groping for my purse,
mindlessly removing the wallet, cosmetics and credit cards and
replacing them. "Does Rick know yet?"
A pause. "No," she'd sighed. "Dr. Mitchell left right
after he got the news. Don't you want to speak to him," she
asked, her voice strained, anxious to end the conversation.
"No. It would be better if he tells Rick first."
"Well. You know what you're doing, I guess. I mean,
he's your brother," she'd said dubiously.
"Yeah. You're sure it's definite?"
"Sure," she'd said, a definitive statement given in a
professionally neutral voice.
"Well, thanks for calling me. Listen, Susan, there's new
drugs and stuff they're working on for this, right? I mean,
anything's possible in terms of a breakthrough, isn't it?"
"Sure, Luce. Anything's possible."
"Even miracles," I'd said, my voice rising with the
intonation of hope.
"Yeah," she'd said flatly. "Even miracles."
There had been no way to be professional with reddened,
bleary eyes, so I drove dry-eyed to the theater, despite a
growing dizziness and nausea. As I checked the props, lights
and wardrobe, I threw up all over the leading man's freshly-
polished wingtip oxfords.

* * * * *

"And he paid full price. It wasn't even on sale," my brother says, beaming into his three-way reflection, snapping me back into the present.

"Yeah. You said."

"It's his way of saying he's sorry I'm sick," Rick said. "Isn't it sharp? I'll wear it tomorrow if the weather's not too cool."

"Yeah. That was really nice of Arty to get it for you. Be careful, though" I say, suspicion chilling my body, "I don't trust him." I wonder if I'll ever feel close to my stepfather.

There was one summer evening I remember when people's curtains were pulled open to admit the slightest ripple of breeze in the moist air, one of those hot nights in Northwest Indiana when the humidity curled everyone's hair and the morning's wash still hung damply on the line. It was just before we started third grade. Rick and I were walking, talking about going to the zoo, maybe the one in Michigan City but preferably Brookfield Zoo, a trip we both loved, but one Arty rarely took us on. My brother had a special eagerness for family outings when we were small, perhaps believing that things would be easier for him and Arty in some different, more public setting than our house. Rick was saying he hoped his father would take us in the fall, maybe after school started. I doubted this. Arty was working six days a week including Monday, Wednesday and Friday evenings. He'd get home around ten, fall on the couch and complain about the long hours he worked, so I figured he wouldn't give up his one day off for a trip to the zoo. On Tuesday and Thursday evenings Arty never worked late in the warmer months, instead coaching the neighborhood softball team that Rick was not a part of, had never tried to join because Arty'd told him not to embarrass him like that.

On our infrequent family outings to the beach, zoo and the Field Museum, Arty occasionally included boys from the team. Once I'd asked to bring a girlfriend along but Arty had looked uneasy so Ma quickly squelched the idea. Rick had never asked to bring anyone and hated those few times when the other boys came along with us. Arty clearly preferred their company to his own son's, walking and talking animatedly with them while Rick hung back on the fringes of the group, filled with resentment and envy.

These thoughts preoccupied me that hot Wednesday evening in August as we wandered to the edge of our neighborhood, where we passed Mrs. Starczyk's front window. The drapes, normally pulled tightly shut, were open in the stifling heat. Rick gasped and froze. I turned to look and stared at the figures of Arty and Mrs. Starczyk, seated on the couch and holding hands. Arty's free hand froze in the act of exploring her exposed thigh, his eyes turned to ours in horror. Rick's face had gone deep red. He'd turned, running back toward our house. I'd followed him, the sound of Mrs. Starczyk's window slamming shut a shattering reverberation in my mind long after its echo left our ears.

At home, the door to Rick's room was closed but I opened it anyway. He was lying face down on his bed, his hands forming fists on the pillow by his head.

"Get out of here," he said savagely. I walked in, quietly trembling, and sat down next to him.

"Get out," he said, but less forcefully.

"Should we tell Mother?" I asked, feeling the pressure of tears and secret knowledge.

"No!" He raised his face, red-blotched and wet. "We mustn't tell anyone. Not ever! Especially Mother. Don't you ever do that to her. Swear to it!"

Dancing to the End   . . . .

We swore secrecy, each of us inflicting a small cut on our wrists with a kitchen knife, then mingling our blood. "Forever blood brother and sister, eternally silent," we solemnly intoned, with Rick's drawings of angels and flowers hanging on the walls surrounding us, bearing witness.

Mrs. Starczyk moved away shortly after. Meanwhile, Arty had bought Mother the new dining room furniture she'd wanted and taken her out to dinner in Chicago. Rick and I figured we knew why and credited that same reason to Arty's unexpected gifts of new bikes for both of us. Even as we rode them, the bikes seemed to us tainted with Arty's guilt.

* * * * *

"What do you mean, you don't trust him?" Rick's hurt now, defensive, and I never meant to do that.

"Arty's disappointed us repeatedly over the years. Every time he's given us anything it was out of guilt."

"Oh, come on, not every time."

"No, not every time. You're right."

* * * * *

To be fair, Arty had some good qualities, especially his unexpectedly comic side when he recalled his childhood to us, so we tried as kids to gauge his moods, testing his willingness and urging him to repeat our favorite stories, which usually included imitations of his small, but apparently, commanding, mother. Arty used to mimic her in his lighter, more nostalgic moments, speaking in a shrill baritone, throwing his hands in the air in mock despair and leaning forward from the hips, shaking the finger of warning, an omen of a bad end.

In one of his stories, Arty remembered being about ten and gulping an orange Popsicle after running around in the heat all afternoon. His mother had always warned him about the danger of eating cold things on a hot stomach, especially Popsicles, which she felt were particularly toxic, no matter what logical evidence to the contrary she was confronted with.

He'd collapsed on the dirty sidewalk, convulsing, his friends crowding around him, screaming, while a neighbor had gone to get his mother. Arty had recovered, waking in the cool darkness of his own room later that afternoon while his mother sat, still and silent, by his bed. She'd looked at him, sighed and said, "It isn't enough. It isn't enough you have no respect, you run with those boys, those hoodlums. It isn't enough you have to stay after school with Sister two days, three days, every week. It isn't enough, God help us, you ask the priest those questions and I have to go talk to him. No. No. You have to give yourself convulsions, too, running around like a nut in the sun, instead of staying cool. And then you go and gulp that ice, that junk, like a pig, and you see? You see what happens? When are you going to be happy, huh? When? When you finally kill yourself and put us both in an early grave, huh? Is that what I deserve?"

That's why Arty irrationally and absolutely vetoed Popsicles, the reason my brother and I grew well past childhood without ever tasting one.

We had never known the grandmother responsible for this ban. Arty's mother had died years before Rick had been born and I had entered his life, so our only picture of her was the pretty, high-collared woman in her twenties that he carried in his wallet and the one he verbally sketched for us of this tiny, forbidding woman, barely five feet tall and 90 pounds, always in black, long-sleeved dresses, no matter how hot and always with the scowl of a widow's anger and disappointment. After a mother like that and ten years of marriage to Iris, Rick's real mother, remembered as a dramatic, brooding woman, my mother must have been a relief to Arty.

He also used to imitate teenagers suffering the consequences of adolescent passion, a spectacle Rick and I found far less amusing, since it was a vehicle for Arty's dire warnings about teenaged sexuality of any sort.

"Plenny-a time for that stuff later on, you're married, then you want a family — that's natural. But no way you wanna get tied down young, not to anyone. Ya play the field, get to know a lotta people, but ya don't play around, or ya find yasself in trouble — big trouble."

He'd hold his hand over his belly, suggesting a pillow-like swelling, whining in a female falsetto, "As God is my witness, I trusted him and now look at me. He said he loved me and now he's gone. I'm stuck like this."

His subtle talents extended to the male half of the hapless, teen duo when he'd lower his voice to a quavering tenor, saying, "Here I am, just 16 and gonna be a dad and stuck inna marriage I don' want. I never wanted this, I just wanted a quick good time."

One March afternoon, Rick came home unusually late, overtly nonchalant in a suspicious way. He must have been about 15 and had been fervently planning the loss of his virginity for some time, preferably with one of the high school football players. Even though this was far more talk than action on Rick's part because of his shyness, it galled me to think he might cross this line into adulthood first. I was so often the pathfinder for the both of us in terms of staying out late, stating my own opinions, in general testing the limits and standing up to Mother and Arty. Of course, I had to be the one to "do it" first, terrifying as that might sometimes seem.

We both worked hard to present ourselves as heterosexual kids to the outside world and Arty and Ma, to everyone but each other, but we knew we were different and so did everyone else. From the time we were in grade school, Rick and I were drawn to people of our own sex, and though we tried to disguise this, our body language and glances revealed us. Often, my brother's girlish mannerisms and lack of interest in sports caused him to be mercilessly teased by the other boys in class. Withdrawn silence and efforts to be invisible were his only defenses, drawing and painting his only outlets for the creativity he mutely attempted to express.

Rick tried to fit in by acting the way he thought a "normal" guy should, trying to overcome his shyness by joining the high school art club. He made sure Ma found a copy of *Playboy* under his bed, while his secret stash of body builder pictures remained well-hidden in the closet under the back stairs and he carried around custom car magazines though his interest in them was limited to their superb paint jobs with extravagant designs.

I was more the free spirit, daring and rebellious, eager to challenge the midwestern mores as the nation broached the '60's new frontiers. At school I flaunted my unconventionality under the guise of intellectual elitism and was quick to accuse others of narrow-mindedness. As we grew away from the other kids, so quick to form boy-girl couples, we found we could talk of our forbidden desires only to each other. We both read a lot and knew there was a larger, more accommodating world at the fringes of our confining neighborhood, calling to us while we were imprisoned in our damp, adolescent purgatories, fantasizing a life of freedom and authentic, unrepressed love. I was the angrier, sometimes reduced to mute, uncomprehending rages at the sight of boy-girl couples, arms around each other's waists in public, so obviously together in a way not only tolerated but encouraged by a society so quick to condemn our feelings.

Rick was eager to report the stories about men in public bathrooms, which always scared me, since he was sensitive and so easily hurt. Even though we were both hormonal teenagers, I was the one to insist that a mutual attraction would be part of a larger, lasting love. While he wistfully agreed, he was quick to entertain the option of unloving, even anonymous, sex for himself, "Just to get it over with that first time. Then move on."

Rick had been talking himself more and more into this frame of mind, growing moodier and somewhat distant, sometimes staying away from home. I missed him and envied him, sensing that he was quietly building a separate, successful life while I, the girl, squirmed under my mother's vigilance. So I was waiting, watching for subtle changes in him.

That cool March afternoon he came home late and flashed me a quick, conspiratal look before dinner, disappearing into the living room to practice the piano without being reminded. That confirmed he'd been up to something, so I cornered him in his room as soon as I could after supper, before he could go out again.

"Okay. What's up?"

"What?" All wide-eyed innocence, sprawled on the bed.

"C'mon. Something happened." Part of me wasn't sure I wanted to find out, though. I had uneasy visions of him groping hotly with another, equally inexperienced boy and Rick seemed so young and uncertain, for all of his cocksure surface around me. Or maybe it had finally happened with somebody older, some thin-haired, paunchy little man who frequented the bus stations and movie theaters we'd heard about. I pictured this predator with pock-marked skin and a dirty, wrinkled raincoat, his practiced oiliness an affront to Rick's fine bones and Cloroxed shirts so carefully ironed. I looked away, rubbing my forehead with the heel of my hand, thinking of my own, not so tentative, desires directed toward the few older girls at school who might appreciate Cole Porter, Virginia Woolfe, Noel Coward, Christopher Isherwood, Gertrude Stein, basketball and another girl's body.

"Nothing happened." He squinted at one of his many pastel pictures tacked on the wall, as though deep into another, far more pressing, thought. He burped loudly, with the portentous rudeness of adolescent rebellion.

Too much. I punched his leg, first testingly, followed by a wind-up to have him seeing colored starlight, but he sat forward, catching my arm in mid-blow. He was fast and strong enough to contain my anger.

"Hey, calm down. No big deal." He released my arm and leaned back against the headboard, drawing his legs under him. He looked at me, all devilish grin and sparkling eyes. "Just best not to talk about it, that's all."

So this was how he wanted to play it. I sat down, untying the shoe lace on his left gym shoe, size 11. "Fine. If that's how you want it. Just be careful, baby brother."

"Yeah, you're so old."

"Older than you."

"By six months, that's all." He shrugged, his casual superiority a shield. Normally, he would have fiercely disputed the age issue, throwing into the equation considerations like wisdom, experience, weight and height. He was already six feet tall and still growing.

"Right. Just be careful."   I sensed something had happened, something significant, so it was my turn to survey the floral designs and portraits he'd drawn, mostly rock stars like Elvis and a few of me and Mother.

"What, be careful? I'm gonna get Jimmy DeLuca pregnant? Or maybe his brother, Bob?" Jimmy and Bobby were the tallest, handsomest boys at school, both decidedly straight, much to my brother's disappointment.

"Not that. The clap. Crabs. Whatever."

He exhaled breath, shaking his head in derision. "Big sister knows so much. Knows nuthin'."

"Fine." I rose to leave. Still three steps from the door, I added casually, "Think Jimmy and Bob would like to know how you dance around in Ma's hat and boa?"

He leaped off the bed, but I put my hand up like a cop, which, curiously, warded him off. "Stop. Right there."

"You wouldn't. Anyway, I only do it once in awhile."

"Doesn't matter. I'll tell. How are you going to face them?" His face, colored with anger, and his glittering, squinty eyes didn't faze me. "And what are you gonna do, Rick? Beat me up, now that you're bigger than me? How are going to explain that to Ma?" Silence.

"Tell." A look, part sheer outrage, but with a flash of something else — relief? Maybe he wanted to tell. He was half smiling, a little light dancing in the back of his eyes.

"Okay, Sis. Maybe you'd better sit down."

"Aren't you being a little dramatic?"

"It *was* pretty dramatic."

I sat on the foot of the bed, waiting, showing him some semblance of jaded sophistication. "Did the earth move?"

He smiled, a superior, knowing leer, settling back into the pillows. He sighed deeply. "Someday, Lucy, you'll meet someone and you'll know it's right, that it's fated to be the two of you. That you'll share something so-o-o special." He lowered his voice to a conspiratorial whisper. "You'll look at her and she'll look at you. And you'll look at her and you'll know and she'll look at you and she'll —"

"Rick!"

"Okay, okay," he agreed with great condescension but I was so eager to hear, I didn't care. "But it will happen for you, too, and —"

"And?"

"And then you'll know."

"And?" The suspense was unbearable.

"And zowie! Wow!"

"Really?" I discarded all pretense of nonchalance. "Who'd you do it with?"

A broad grin and a moment of silence — a very long moment — for effect. "Jim." Another pause. "The one and only Big Jimbo."

"Jimmy DeLuca?" I couldn't believe it.

The smile settled into one of pleased lechery. "Yeah." He sighed with contentment, leaning back into the pillows. "He was great. Really great."

"No!"

"Yeah. We took turns."

"You did? What did you do?"

A patronizing smile. "Told ya. Took turns. Man, what a tongue on him." Clearly, he was delighted with himself and his own vulgarity, which was maddening. Another satisfied sigh, deeper than the other. "And it was perfect, just the right size. And color — man, I'll never forget that shade of purple, as God is my witness, I swear I won't, never 'til my dying day." He solemnly placed his hand over his chest. "Never." He doubled up on the bed, laughing.

"Rick." He couldn't talk any more, he was laughing so hard. *"Rick!"*

"It was great —" He stopped for a moment, laughing breathlessly. "So great. And big and hard." Still more laughter. "And pur... and purple!"

He rolled over on his back, doubled over, grabbing his sides. "It was...it was the best, big sister...and there we were, taking turns...me and Jim...licking and licking...that big, luscious... pur...purple...*POPSICLE!"*

"A what?"

More gasping. "A Popsicle. I had one with Jimmy. It was great, like you can't imagine. My first one."

"A Popsicle? A lousy Popsicle!"

He sat up, gleeful and triumphant. "Right. It was grape. So purple," and he started to laugh again. "Man, I really had you going, didn't I?"

I pounded the bed with my fist. "Jesus, Rick, a stinking, lousy Popsicle. I really thought —"

"I know what you thought," he said, still laughing so hard he couldn't stop, and his glee cut through my outraged disappointment and relief so that I couldn't contain my own laughter, sputtering irrepressibly from me. We wound up howling together, holding our stomachs and rolling on the bed, simple and absurd as the two kids we were then.

December, 1985 — CHICORY COFFEE

*T*he sign on his door screams "Special Precautions" in large red letters, insisting his garbage must be burned and forbidding direct human contact with any part of his body. With rubber gloves on, I am allowed to touch his door knob, carefully balancing my large commuter mug filled with rich, dark chicory coffee.

As usual before entering Rick's room, I'm wearing a surgical gown, struggling with my surgical mask, wondering if I should have put that on first instead of the cap, but refusing to pull the whole apparatus off to start again. At least I'm doing the rubber gloves last. Tying a surgical cap with gloves on is tough for me, as is the rest of this ritual with sterile surgical gown and mask.

The floor of this hospital wing is hushed on early Sunday mornings and I occasionally visit Rick on the spur of the moment then, knowing we can just be together quietly for awhile before anyone else comes by.

The nurses and aides have recently come on duty at such times, some drinking coffee to wake up and some who work 16-hour shifts taking large swallows of it, strong and black, just to remain on their feet. I force a smile, remembering through the tight grin the threats needed to make them set foot in Rick's room, let alone care for him.

Dancing to the End . . . .

It was the only time I'd ever used my press credentials for personal reasons.

"It's very simple, Mr. Michalik," I'd said nine months ago on a sunny afternoon, sitting across from him at his large walnut desk. Our mood was anything but cordial.

"You know as well as I do that the nurses and aides avoid my brother's room, yet he's here in the hospital to be cared for by professionals and the insurance is paying for that."

Michalik interlaced his fingers and sighed, glancing at the jet pen and pencil set on his right. For a tense moment, neither of us spoke. I took advantage of those few seconds to scrutinize the carefully-furnished office, complete with no-color beige wall-to-wall carpeting, ivory drapes, tan leather chairs and a few careless touches of gray used for accent here and there. I wondered if these were his choices.

"My family," I continued, "does the actual, hands-on care for everything other than technical things, since the nursing staff won't. We carry his food trays in and out, get him extra blankets, you name it. I think the insurance company and the public's got the right to know that Northwest Indiana's first AIDS case has been hospitalized here — and will be going elsewhere, due to inadequate care."

His full, dark eyebrows shifted closer together and his mouth narrowed as he said, "I assure you that your brother is receiving the best care that any health facility can provide. Here at St. John's Hospital, patient care is our number one concern and always has been. In fact, this institution has long been known for its tender, loving care."

I remained silent, staring.

He continued, coughing softly, "This is a situation of great delicacy and concern to all of us. Although AIDS has only been around a few years, we in the medical profession have accumulated a significant body of data on this condition and have certain protocols and procedures which we follow closely."

He rattled some loose papers on his desk for emphasis. "What makes you so certain your brother's not getting the care he needs?"

I listened, marshalling my facts to focus on the issue at hand, realizing I'd been telegraphing my nervousness to Michalik by picking at the lint on the left sleeve of my blouse.

"The family's doing the routine maintenance chores for Rick but my brother needs nursing professionals checking him regularly, not an occasional head in the doorway. The only time there's evidence of nurses in there is to hook up a new IV. Then they're out of there until the next IV."

"You do understand —" Michalik started.

"I understand my brother needs professional medical attention and he's not getting it," I interrupted. "Yesterday I came by to see him and he was asleep, lying in his own blood, all over his face, his neck, the sheets. I woke him and he told me he'd had a bad nosebleed. He'd rung for a nurse but nobody came in to see about it. I cleaned him up myself."

My voice came from deep inside, from a buried, hidden place, but still I continued, driven by an immeasurable, bottomless force. "This is inexcusable and intolerable."

He'd said nothing, which had the effect of goading me on. "If no one here cares, maybe someone out there does and the public's got the right to know."

"And what makes you think anyone in the press would listen to you or take these charges seriously?" he asked, arching his left eyebrow at me.

Removing a small, plastic-laminated card from my breast pocket, I gripped the edges tightly and extended it towards him, so he could see the bright red letters spelling out "Press Pass" and my ID photo from *The Herald,* the paper I'm with.

"The Center for Disease Control in Atlanta is very clear about the rubber gloves to protect him against infectious secondary invaders, the whole thing. And people can't have contact with his bodily fluids. I understand that." I paused for breath to continue. "But the fact remains, my brother needs to have professional medical personnel checking on him regularly, not just an occasional head in the doorway or a nurse every time he needs a shot."

He half rose, his hands separated, palms down on the desk. "What makes you the medical expert here?"

"It's not technical expertise. It's common sense — the conventional wisdom that all patients, including the terminally ill, do better with caring attention than without. If my brother didn't have family, he'd definitely be without here at St. John's. Because here he's neglected by so-called professionals who lack not only basic common sense, but common decency as well."

His eyes narrowed to dark, thin lines as he stood, looming silently over me, his body tense with the effort to intimidate.

"You can't frighten me and you can't silence me," I said, despite the fear I felt at this dark, threatening man, trying to stare him down. "Quite simply, my family and I have nothing to lose."

He looked down, exhaling a long breath. The unadorned truth of that statement hung in the air mutely between us.

Frightened and spent, I snatched my purse and left the office with great, long strides. I didn't close the door, continuing down the tiled floor towards the exit. When I reached my navy Toyota, I flung my body into the gray seat, trembling, sobs rising and overtaking me, shaking and choking me, smothering any last remaining hope I held for the human race.

* * * * *

Mother was furious when I told her. She has always stood in awe of doctors and priests, nodding at everything they said when she has been with them, sometimes repeating key words in a tiny, frightened voice. But she's the first to say she doesn't believe any of them as soon as they're out of earshot.

Michalik called all of us — Mother, Arty and me — into his office the afternoon after my confrontation with him. Arty gave him a big smile and a handshake and it was clear he and Michalik would deal with this issue man-to-man.

Directing the conversation to Arty, Michalik said, "Mr. Salaski, there seems to be some unfortunate misunderstanding about your son, Richard."

"Yes?" Arty listened intently.

"Your daughter —"

"Stepdaughter."

"Yes, she has implied to me that this hospital is at fault with your son's medical care. While no institution is 100% perfect, I'm sure you can understand that every procedure we take here is for Richard's own good. We realize people who are not in the medical professions may sometimes jump to erroneous conclusions without an adequate factual base and we understand." He flashed a large smile at Arty.

"Of course, of course," Arty nodded rapid agreement, hanging on every word. Mother simply nodded once, a barely visible motion.

"I'm sure you'll agree that no one, your stepdaughter included, can try to intimidate us with a threat about public disclosure of patient neglect, which is a very serious charge." Michalik looked grim, shaking his head. "A very serious charge," he repeated sadly, "especially coming from someone who is supposed to be a professional, a member of the professional press corps."

"No, no, she can't do that." Arty's head almost twisted off his neck from all the swiveling left to right. I felt the blood throbbing in my head, an angry, metallic taste filling my mouth. I wanted to spit. The throbbing in my head rose to a roar, but it couldn't stop me.

"Bullshit," I began.

Michalik cut in, "I think Jake Thompson will agree when I see him today that his people cast themselves and the paper in a dubious light if I tell him of our meetings."

John T. "Jake" Thompson III owns and publishes *The Herald.* The metallic taste in my mouth sharpened. I felt myself unable to control the rising heat on my face as Michalik continued, clearing his throat for emphasis.

"When you stop to consider the number of patients we at St. John's care for at any given time, you certainly can see that our hospital procedure can't be dictated by the needs of a single patient, no matter how concerned his family may be or how serious the affliction."

"Fine," I said sarcastically, rising to leave. "I hate to think of a hospital being inconvenienced by patient needs, after all," I threw back, "Especially when you told me just yesterday that patient needs were the number one concern here at St. John's."

No longer quiet, Mother hissed from her chair, "For God's sake Lucy, sit down and shut up."

"Every patient here is assured of the finest medical care available," Michalik said stiffly, scratching at his right temple in frustration. I saw the large circle of perspiration wetting his pale blue oxford shirt at the armpit. His flush was a combination of anger and embarrassment.

"Except for fags with AIDS," I interrupted. Arty waved his hand at me frantically to shut up and I sat down.

"Look, this is not easy for any of us at St. John's," Michalik said, scanning the room with his dark blue eyes. I gave him silence.

He paused, searching Arty's face for some shred of agreement, but Arty looked away. I didn't speak, feeling the tension thicken in the carpeted room.

Mother licked her lips. Her face was very pale, with small patches of high color beneath her washed-out eyes. The fingers of her left hand trembled slightly while she fingered her old, ebony rosary beads, hand-carved by her grandfather. "She's right, you know. If it weren't for us here almost all the time, he'd have no one to help him." Mother was forcing his attention with her frailty.

"We come here and do what we can, but what we have to go through to get a bed changed or anything. You speak to this aide or that one, or to a nurse, but all they do is nod, or at the most, write it down, but it doesn't get done and an hour later you're saying the same things all over again." Now she was facing Michalik's eyes directly. "It's not just a matter of them being busy, because they manage to make it into other patients' rooms. But not my son's. Not when we need them. Three days ago, they put his IVs back in when they pulled out, but the sheets were all wet from the antibiotic that had leaked and my husband and I wound up changing the bed ourselves, and we both have weak hearts and bad backs. What if something had happened to us while we were doing *your* people's work?"

Arty just sank more deeply into the chair, pale against the black leather.

Small droplets of moisture were forming on Michalik's head. This pleased me until I became aware of matching drops on my own.

"Clearly, there's been a misunderstanding here, Mrs. Salaski." Michalik's tone turned placating. "I've checked with our doctors. They assure me all the proper procedures have been attended to on a timely basis. I understand your concern, but you're not a professional, after all. You can rest assured your family member is getting proper care and please, please, don't ever undertake changing a bed or anything like that again. I will personally guarantee his care, Mrs. Salaski."

Mother's voice took on an edge as cutting as her look. "You're a man of your word?"

Michalik flashed the smile made perfect by orthodontia, reminding me of the white tiles in Rick's hospital bathroom. "Of course," he said proudly. "Our staff is the best in the area and do their best for each patient, irregardless of their condition."

"Regardless?" I corrected, unable to resist.

"Yes," he insisted, adding for emphasis, this time in my direction, "Regardless!"

"Do we have your word that care will never be an issue again?" I persisted.

"It never was," he said, with his neck rigid, facing Arty.

"All right. That's settled. Let's go," Arty sighed, getting out of the deep chair. As I rose to leave, I resented the male assumption that this official closure of negotiations be left to them. I didn't want to drop it because I wanted to be the one to end it. But I knew I had to and did for my brother's sake, since he was what the whole thing had been about, after all.

After that, hospital staff entered Rick's room regularly, though they hated it in the beginning. They collected in the hall outside his room or by the nurses' station, complaining like malevolent blood clots, shooting me looks and raising their voices whenever I walked by so I couldn't miss the hissed hostility of their whispers. Once, a particularly insulting LPN stared, stage whispering something about "...that fag ... and his dyke sister."

I ignored the congregation, focusing my attention on that nurse, lewdly eyeing her lumpen body and walking down the hall, hearing the orderlies whistle and hoot while the nurses tried to quiet them.

Later, I asked Mother if she'd ever heard the staff whispering about either of us, but she just stared blankly out the window, answering "No" in a flat tone. After some time she turned to me, lips narrow and barely moving as she said in her serious tone used only for important family business, "Don't you go starting with that mouth of yours, you hear? They'll only wind up taking it out on your brother. He'll be the one who suffers for it in the end."

She was right, so I brought three dozen homemade chocolate chip cookies to the evening staff later that day, along with humility and walnut fudge brownies to the day crew the following afternoon. It wasn't easy for me. Throughout that week I mentally replayed the situation, teeth clenched with anger and pride, but whenever Rick's hospitalized now, whether for two days, three, a week or more, I am the "goodie lady" for the staff, all smiles, killing them with kindness, good cheer and some special homemade treat loaded with extra calories and cholesterol. The hefty LPN has grown noticeably more lumpen and the issue of sexual orientation, neither mine nor my brother's, is ever discussed, at least not around me.

Gradually, the staff has adjusted to Rick's situation and now it's sometimes hard to get the nurses out of my brother's room. Rick asks them about their families, tells jokes and laughs at the stories they tell him. Sometimes his old humor sparks. "Rita, those eyes, those lips, that hair. You're the most beautiful aide here today, almost competition for me," he says, looking like a pale octopus socket, connected to yards of plastic IV tubing.

Ironically, he makes *them* feel good, makes them giggle, even the ones who'd initially feared him, so they love him now and try to be noticed and praised by him. He celebrates the snacks the aides carry to him every few hours as though they'd personally prepared them.

"My God, you've done it again, Sylvie. You make a plain egg something special."

Sylvie, a large fading blonde, blushes to her roots at this, beaming with thanks and pleasure.

*   *   *   *   *

When I come in this morning, the room has no nurses. Rick is leaning into his pillows.

"Oh, hi. It's rainy today. I'm glad you're here." He yawns, and turning off the small red Walkman by his side, pulls the earplug from his right ear and puts the apparatus on the metal nightstand to the right of his bed. There's barely room for the small radio since Rick's arranged some family photos on it, along with a small bear pocket fetish carved of pipestone that I bought him in Santa Fe. Mother's added a statuette of Jesus, "so they know we're holy."

He hasn't told her the Zuni bear carving is more than a simple animal figurine, that the use of fetishes dates to pre-Columbian times. Native Americans are not the only ones who use fetishes, believing they house the spirit or supernatural qualities of that animal. May the bear's ferocious courage rub off on Rick, on all of us. The difference between a figurine and a fetish is a matter of faith.

The rest of the room is standard-issue nondescript, with oatmeal drapes, ivory walls and one picture, a bland landscape of a windmill in a field. The visitors' chairs are upholstered in bright orange fabric, providing the only real color in the place, such a contrast to my own, brightly-decorated home, one of the rare adobe houses in Chicago's south suburban area. It took me two years to find it. Inside, my hand-painted ceremonial drum heads from Taos hang on the walls next to cow skulls and framed posters of Native American pottery and Georgia O'Keeffe paintings. In my kitchen, to the right of a small Navaho rug, hangs a poster of an unconscious woman in silver and turquoise jewelry and cowboy boots, lying on an Indian rug and surrounded by every southwestern artifact imaginable. It's captioned "Another Victim of the Santa Fe Style." After all, if I can't spoof myself, who can?

He yawns again, deeply, sitting up straighter against his pillows but carefully, to avoid disturbing his sketch pad and charcoal sticks or the IV dripping into his arm. Although his forearm is taped to a rigid board, his IVs still pull out when he tosses restlessly in his dreams.

"Hi, Honey. How's it going today? Are you feeling okay?" I yawn. "Thought I'd come by early." An edgy, nervous energy often makes sleep elusive for me these days. I take the soft arm chair by the north window where the cool, filtered light of early morning comes in through the slats of the ivory mini-blinds. Setting my mug down, I recall Maureen's deep brown eyes, intent on pouring me that coffee less than an hour ago. I'd hated leaving her warm smile and easy laughter for the cold car ride to the hospital with its sterile procedures and attitudes.

"Guess what?" Rick smiles, eager with secrets he can't hold.

"You're pregnant," I try sarcastically.

He screws his forehead in mock seriousness. "No, but the doctor says if I really keep trying —"

I get too scared and impatient in hospitals to kid around much. He looks really pale this morning, which only makes my nerves worse. "What is it, really?"

He looks at me with surprise and concern. "You okay?"

"Sure. Why?"

"You look nervous, jittery, like you didn't sleep. I hope you at least had a good reason for losing sleep." He arches one eyebrow, lewdly.

"No," I say lightly, hoping my face doesn't telegraph the correctness of his guess. His love life may never again be more than memories and I don't want to say anything to remind him of that loss. "Hey, tell me your surprise."

He savors the taste of his news. I can imagine his forming every word with slow care, letter by letter, moist inside his mouth, safely away from the cold sores on his lips. "If my temp stays normal for another day, I can go home."

I sit forward, excited. Home. Away from this hospital. "Good. Good, that's great. Have you told anyone yet?"

"Just you so far," he grins. "Something could go wrong."

"When will you know?"

"Probably tomorrow morning. Really, I'm ready to go now. In fact, if I can just convince them I feel fine, I don't see why they can't let me out today." There's a note of the petulant child in his voice.

I understand Rick hates being in the hospital, but I also know how sick he can be and the care he requires. He has an ability to forget that most of the time, until the next round of deep, harsh coughing of yet another pneumonia overtakes him as he struggles for breath, or another gushing nosebleed refuses to be stanched by the application of mere ice. But laughing now, only too glad to dismiss these grim images, I reassure him, "I'll cross all my fingers and toes and hope."

He says in a new tone, a serious tone, "We talked to him."

"Who?"

"The doctor. Ziti, Dr. Ziti. We fixed it up with him so that he'll take care of me." Rick's face colors.

"Take care of you? Doesn't he take care of you now?" I feel stupid.

"You know." He can't meet my eyes.

"No, I honestly don't. Please, just spell it out for me."

He pauses, seeming to reach inward for some strength to sustain him through this. After several long moments of silence, he speaks. "At the end — when it's going to happen." His voice is hard and flat. "He'll make sure I'm comfortable and don't suffer."

I can't speak for a moment. "Just exactly what are you saying? That he's going to kill you?"

"No, he can't do that!" His flush deepens to scarlet.

"You asked him?" My head starts to throb.

Rick looks at me quietly.

I pierce the silence insistently. "C'mon, Rick, did you or did you not ask him to kill you?"

His voice rises. "Not in so many words, but yes, I asked him."

"Jesus Christ. You asked a doctor to kill you?" Wondering if ignorance of this wouldn't have been preferable, I lean back into the support of the chair.

"Well, he said his oath of office, whatever it is that they swear to, wouldn't allow him to take a life, no matter what."

"And you didn't know that? Jesus Christ!" I push my fingers through the hair I'd so carefully combed earlier that morning, looking down.

"Sure I did. Yes."

"Then why did you ask him, Rick," I ask, lifting my eyes and facing him squarely. "Didn't you think?"

His face resumes its normal paleness. "We thought —"

"Wait a minute, just who is this 'we?' "

He glances away, toward the window. "Never mind."

"Rick, don't do that! I swear, you make me so crazy when you do that! You can't start something like this and just expect me to drop it!"

"Well, do," he says, his voice flat and definite.

"What?" I return his challenge with defiance.

"Drop it, Lucy."

"I won't. We stare at each other, furiously deadlocked.

"Okay." He looks down at the white sheets, then into my eyes. "My father and I — it wasn't so much that we asked him that. I didn't say it right. It's more about the suffering at the end. He'll make sure I don't feel much. It won't hurt. Dad was his softball coach, you know, so it wasn't hard for them to talk." He pauses, looking away, apparently mulling it over. "Frankly, I'm grateful now he's known Ziti so long."

He looks at me directly. "You know I can't take pain. And sometimes, in these cases, the brain goes first. You can imagine that. And besides," he says, eyes pleading, "you know I'm a big baby."

"So what is he going to do?"

"Not much, really," Rick says off-handedly, trying to minimize the issue. "Just make sure I get the right kind of pain killers and plenty of them when the time comes."

"And that will keep you comfortable? But why did you have to make such an issue of it with him? Isn't that what he's supposed to do, anyway?"

"Rick flushes again, looking away. "Yeah, sure. But there's degrees, levels, you know?"

"I guess I don't," I say softly, withdrawing into myself to ponder this development.

"He'll make sure I stay sort of floaty. Like I'll be here, but I won't; I'll just be totally out of it and above it all. And that's really more than he has to do."

I catch myself starting to rummage in my purse for a cigarette even though I quit more than a month ago. In a way, this direct discussion is a relief. I've heard about AIDS patients suffering at the end, wasting away, weakly trying to fight through mucous-clogged lungs for air. There is dementia and hemorrhaging in some cases. Maybe this is the best way.

So Rick's coming home, but not today. When he's home it's impossible to know if it will be for a day, a week or even a month or two, just as it's impossible to know when this or any other home-coming may be his last.

The door swings open into Rick's room and Mother walks in, neatly capped, gowned and masked. She stops abruptly, seeing me.

115

"Lucy, if only I'd known you would be coming over this early! I could have done my cooking this morning, gotten that all out of the way and then gone to a wake this afternoon! How I wish I'd known, then I could have come here later. It's old Mrs. Vacek's mother and I wanted to stop by that wake."

"To round out your day."

"Oh, don't be like that, Lucy! So disrespectful! With you, so much is a joke — too much. Someday you'll know!"

"I think I do already, Ma."

"Not you, with that attitude. That isn't nice. So I won't talk to you, so there. So I'll talk to Rick." She nods decisively, turning to face him. "You doing any better?"

"A little, yeah." He grins, whether at my conversation with Mother or in welcome to her, I don't know. "I'm fine, really. Glad you're here."

"You want something?" Mother asks, anxious to perform some task, any action she can view as beneficial. "Some juice? You had breakfast?"

"A little while ago. Oatmeal."

"You ate it?"

"Yes." His pale face is bland as oatmeal.

"Good, 'cause you should; it's good for you. Just oatmeal?"

"No."

"What, then? Tell me," she coaxes, as one would a toddler.

He sighs, then ticks off the litany of food, a ritual he's grown used to. "There was also juice, coffee, toast and fruit."

"You ate it all I hope?"

"I ate most of it." Rick's voice takes on a warning tone.

116

"Most of it? What do you mean, most of it?" She recites her portion of this script faithfully, still investing hope in the curative powers of good food and bed rest.

"I ate what I could, okay, Ma?" Rick says, his voice rising in irritation. "I'm not a child. I ate until I was full."

"Oh, I don't know; you've got to eat." She turns toward me. "How long have you been here? Did you see him eat," she asks accusingly, as though I'd been negligent in performing this duty, albeit unassigned.

"Ma, for God's sake!"

"Just answer me, Lucy. Did you or did you not see him eat his breakfast?"

She stares accusingly into my eyes. "I wasn't here when they brought breakfast." As I say this, I realize there's no sign of any breakfast having been brought in, no tray, cups, plates — nothing. I know Rick doesn't like to be nagged about eating even though he loves to talk about choosing and preparing food, but I sense something's wrong and find myself turning my head, glancing toward him questioningly.

"I ate early. Hours ago." He chews his lower lip, refusing to meet my eyes. That only happens when he needs extra pain shots or pills, which are taken with food. This means his pain was worse and the late-night medication didn't last him 'til morning, as it has.

"It must have been really early." I hear fear in my voice.

He glances out the window. "About 4:30."

"They gave you breakfast at 4:30 in the morning?" Mother's mouth remains half-open.

"I had some trouble sleeping and got hungry, so I asked for some breakfast early," he snaps, hating to admit his pain, especially to Mother, who cries so easily these days.

"They made you oatmeal at 4:30?" For a moment, Mother is delighted at the prospect of such special treatment, completely blocking its implication from her consciousness, but she narrows her eyes at Rick in suspicion and concern.

"Instant. They made instant."

"Oh." Her face sags.

I glance out the window, preferring to lose myself in the sight of the slanting, icy rain for a moment as they pursue the virtues of instant versus scratch oatmeal. The rain splashes in the puddles left from last night's thunderstorm.

* * * * *

There had been the walk yesterday with Maureen, over the gray, barren field less than an hour's drive from Chicago, down the water-etched gullies of the ravine to the canyon-like area below; then introductions to Michael, the Firetender, who was carefully arranging the wood as the late afternoon shadows lengthened into dusk. He complimented me on my T-shirt with its large drawing of a turquoise bear fetish against a black background, worn especially for this occasion. When all ten of us were there, we shared in the ritual lighting of the fire, followed by a wait in the deepening night until the stones were hot enough. I removed my shoes, socks, jacket and all metal objects before crawling into the tiny sweat lodge and sitting on the cold, damp earth. Maureen sat outside because of her asthma, meditating and leaning against the lodge to share energy with us while Michael remained by the fire. Inside, the seven others laughed when I'd shivered in my thin cotton jeans and bear shirt, reminding me it would warm up soon enough.

They weren't kidding. As the hot stones were added one by one to the fire pit, we collectively honored them, the spirits of our ancestors. The steam and temperature rose, hot, hotter, then hotter still as some in the tiny lodge bent close to the cooler air near the earth, covering their heads with blankets or towels to trap that blessed air. I didn't know which was harder to bear — the gusts of steam as water and sage were periodically sprinkled on the stones or the more subtle, all-pervasive heat that threatened to etch holes in my bursting lungs. I resolved to see it through, reminding myself that this was, after all, a rigorous purification ceremony.

I was rocking back and forth to the rhythm of the chanting and songs, gasping for breath with my mouth open, sitting on the earth squeezed between Lois and John, when the vision engulfed me.

It was the abyss. The vision I'd so steadfastly held — of soulmates, kindred spirits, spirit sisters united in every way, in a total relationship — was crashing to earth, burning to ashes. Christina's anguished face floated before me, promising so much, and I thought of her trying to erase the memories of my touch with the hands of others. A shudder rippled throughout my body and the hairs on my arms stood on end.

Doubled over, I clutched my arms around my midsection, rocking slightly. Still the abyss swirled around me and still I continued to clutch and protect. My breathing and heart beat raced in the face of the darkness before me. I felt myself surrounded by the bottomless chaos of an abyss without sides, without dimensions or parameters of any kind. More and more I looked into it, at first with a nameless, unspeakable primal terror unable to be contained, then gradually with lessening fear until I felt only mild fright, then the beginnings of relaxation and finally, amazingly, comfort with the dimensionless emptiness. My whole self let go and sank gracefully, gratefully, surrendering to that endless void.

Wondrously, I did not fall, but drifted lightly into its almost palpable mass, held by it, supported on soft, supporting currents of air and energy. It carried me deeper into itself, into myself, sustaining me effortlessly.

My breathing and heart beat slowed and I saw an image of myself as some sort of winged knight, yet unmistakably myself, leaving the earth and flying through the clouds, Maureen flying with me. I saw that I had my arm around her waist, helping support her efforts to penetrate the skies. I looked into Maureen's handsome, high cheekboned face, seeing it shift and change, becoming the features of Ed, the young Ed I'd loved and married so many years ago, Ed with the bright blue eyes sparkling with intensity. It altered, becoming the face of Sharon, the one I'd loved so much and so long ago, all beautiful, frank brown eyes and a quizzical look around the mouth and after that, I found myself looking into Christina's inscrutable, deep gray eyes. The face changed yet again to Rick's, crinkled with laughter, then to my daughter Julie's, so like my own with that look of need mixed with doubt. The face once again became Christina's, inexplicably drawn with grief.

It was at that moment I first felt, then looked down and saw, my legs becoming sharp-ended, topped by tufts of feathers, my arms billowing out with long wing tips as I swept higher, higher, my mouth becoming beaked, open with joy as the shrill cry of a white-tailed hawk left my ruffled throat. I felt the upsurges against my wings, steadied my feathered weight to catch them and was swept on the air currents to yet another, higher level. I looked down at Christina, held gently in my long talons and saw that she was holding a baby with blond-white hair, the image of Ed as an infant.

"I'm sorry," I said, "But I have to let you go. I have to let all of you go. I love you and it isn't you, it's me — I can't fly higher if I take you along."

The look of grief intensified on the woman's face, which became Ed's saying, "Honest to God, Lucy, don't go. Please don't go, Luce," that night I'd left him and our marriage 12 years ago. Then it changed into Sharon's face saying, "Why must it be this way? Can't I still know you?"

Finally, the face once again became Christina's, thinly veneered with a socially-acceptable level of a flip, take-charge independence betrayed only by the tiny crack in her voice, saying, "Can we be platonic friends? Can we try? Should I call you in say, a month? Six months? No. Never mind. Forget it. Bad idea."

"I can't do it. I'm so, so sorry," I said to them all. "I have to fly higher." I saw for the first time what others saw in me, what so many found frightening — that driving force to push on, faster, higher, no matter what the obstacles, that spirit-driven vision to cut through the wind and sky — and realized I could be seen as ruthlessly cold and that others could easily resent me for this sharply-focused passion.

"I have to go now," I said to Christina. "I loved you, but I have to let you go so I can fly," and I gently loosened my hold on the woman and child who fell, turning and tumbling away through the clouds with a thin cry.

Released from my burden, I turned my head skyward and glided effortlessly, lightly, up one thermal current then another, soaring deeper into the light. I looked down on the faces and lives below, seeing Ed, Christina, Maureen, Rick, Sharon, Mother, all of them, even Julie in college on the East

Coast. I passed over the diminishing rivers and mountains, drawing nearer and nearer to the brightness.

Flying close enough to touch the edge of the sun's swirling gasses, I paused and heard or felt a voice say, "You've done it. You've flown into the sun. Now can you do the rest?"

Without hesitation, I folded my wings and stepped lightly into the star stream. I felt myself hurled through space, time, timelessness and emptiness, painlessly disintegrating, feathers, claws, beak, flesh, intestines, until finally I was vaporized into part of the air currents, part of the swirling cosmos of pure light energy.

My vaporous particles scattered throughout whirling, streaming currents of brightness, without discernible speed or movement, through a vast, dimensionless swirl of being.

Then I was soaring lower, much lower, back into the earth's wind currents, once again a hawk high above the surface, calling over and over, "I am! I am!" covering mile after mile, gradually slowing and drawing nearer to the ground. After awhile, I landed in the uppermost branches of a tree in northern New Mexico, folded my wings and looked down at the dark haired woman with the long, loose curls who stood beneath me, holding pen and paper in her hand and gazing upward intently. I ruffled my feathers and rested.

Gradually, I heard the chanting, felt the stabbing heat in my lungs and the confinement of the tiny, dark lodge packed with bodies. The two-hour ceremony ended and the others helped me out into the sharp, cold bite of the outside air, since I could not walk. Maureen and John half-carried me around to the back of the lodge, gently laying me on the dewy ground while steam left my body, rising, as the sounds of a building thunderstorm drew nearer. Despite the cold, damp earth, I wasn't chilly, but comfortably and peacefully supported by the ground beneath me and the sky above. Maureen stayed with me, rubbing my hands in hers as if they'd been frostbitten rather than steamed, all the while speaking to me about my family, my poetry and our plans for the coming weekend, talking me back to this earthly plane.

I returned to her deeply moved, knowing that I had not been asleep and dreaming, nor had I been hallucinating. I was certain I'd never before experienced this type of altered consciousness and knew I had been profoundly changed by the experience, able to see myself differently, for the first time understanding those who saw my capacity for a single-minded, courageous intensity as bordering on the ferocious. I understood that my brief, infrequent and anguishing glimpses of flight with a kindred spirit-soul into the sun were simply that — glimpses, and not real possibilities for me. After a break-up with a real or potential soulmate, after grieving the inevitable heartbreak, ultimately I'd found an updraft, a shaft of light, an air current to help me soar higher, clearer, purer — and alone.

For me, I realized, it was a choice between that: either the pure ecstacy of unencumbered flight or a slow process of fading away. I knew I could never love another human being as much as I could love this dream, this exaltation of the ultimate solo flight.

The sound of the storm grew nearer. Maureen helped me stand on wobbly legs, easing me into my jacket and supporting my first few unsteady steps. Suddenly, I was cold, not just cold and wet, but shiveringly, bone chillingly freezing. She led me to the remains of the fire where Michael, Lois, John and the others were talking. They'd been to sweats before and had changed into the extra dry clothes they'd brought, some wrapped in dry blankets as well. My legs were still weak but Maureen held me lightly, supporting me, quiet in the circle as we shared the berries and salmon the others passed around.

"When I meditated, I felt the stars above and a deep energy inside me," she told me softly, her dark eyes glistening, reflecting the glow of the embers, "and your spirit through the wall — together." My uncontrollable shivering persisted. I could not speak. Maureen smiled and lowered her head, shaking it from side to side, repeating, "Lucy, Lucy, Lucy," something she often did when feeling overwhelmed by emotion. She swiftly leaned into me, kissing me lightly on my forehead. "I'm so proud of you," she whispered to me. Removing the scarf from her neck, she wrapped it around my upturned collar and bent to help me on with my socks and sneakers, tying the bow not once but twice.

"You double-knotted my shoes," I said, wonderingly, feeling a physical sensation of love for her surge in my chest.

"Of course," she said, smiling. "I made sure they weren't going anywhere," and she squeezed my arm, helping me toward the slope of the ravine as the thunder rumbled and the first raindrops fell.

*   *   *   *   *

"...And you know what's a good way to fix it? I'd never had it like that before —" Abruptly, I realize I'm sitting in the hospital chair while the two of them talk about food.

"Where'd you have pot roast like that, Rick? When," Mother asks sharply, her mouth compressing in disapproval.

"Oh, a while ago. I just remember it, is all." Maybe it's not a good topic and not such a good way to fix it, after all.

"Who made it for you?" There's no disguising the edge in her voice.

"Nobody." Once again he is bland as oatmeal.

"Nobody?" She presses.

"No one special. Just a friend I knew."

"Oh." Mother knows better than to press the issue, preferring not to imagine a series of smiling men in aprons fixing pot roasts for her son.

"Not fixed with glazed carrots like I make them, nice, you know the way I cut them, with the fancy edges, all crinkle-cut."

He tries to placate her. "No, Ma, not with your carrots."

"No. No. Of course not. No one makes carrots like I make my carrots." Relieved, she turns to me, glances at the old riding boots and breeches visible beneath the edge of my hospital gown. "You going out to ride your horse?"

"Yeah. I should leave for the barn now, as a matter of fact."

"Well." She sighs. "It's cold, awful cold and damp. You don't want to wait until later this morning when it warms up a little?" Mother's wheedling, wanting me to stay. She wants to run home and do her cooking in peace while Arty's ushering at church; then she can change her clothes and still pick up the wake this afternoon.

She wants to go, but doesn't want Rick alone for a long stretch of the day. I don't want that either but sometimes he is alone, even on evenings and weekends, sometimes especially on evenings and weekends, simply for the rest of us to maintain the sanity of lives separate from hospital procedures and routine.

"No. I'll go now. By the time I pick Cherokee's stall I'll be warm, believe me."

"I don't know why you pay to board that horse of yours if you go cleaning his stall every time you go out there. They do that every day for the horses."

"They do. But I like to keep it nice and clean for him." There's a feeling of solid achievement that comes with cleaning stalls. "For the short time it's clean, it makes me happy."

"Horses." She sighs, looks towards the window then down at her reddened hands. "When I was 18 my girlfriend and I used to get all dressed up with our cowboy hats and boots and our riding gloves and the big leather belts with the buckles and go riding two, three Sundays a month in the good weather. We'd ride all over." She finds my eye. "I don't like you riding out on the trails all alone. You know better."

"I know. I won't," I say, knowing I will, knowing that setting off alone, just Cherokee and me, is one of the main reasons I ride. Increasingly, I'm drawn to the compelling solitude of our rides, the ease that comes from our long time understanding of each other, the companionship when horse and rider blend into a single, old friend.

There is the special camaraderie and humor shared with my barn friends as we wash and groom our horses together but the dearest friend I see at the barn is my horse, Cherokee. The time I spend with him is my best, most relaxed time for thinking things through or just being. I let myself be real with him; I let him know me.

Rick understands that this half-ton animal has often been what's kept me going. Maybe some day Maureen will, too. I'd like to bring Maureen to the stable one day so she could meet my horse. She hasn't ridden in years, not since she was a kid and used to ride a friend's horse bareback through fields that were eventually developed into the estate-sized homes that added so significantly to her family's fortune. Now the fields are just a memory for her.

My brother hasn't been able to visit the barn with me for awhile, but he used to enjoy it. As children we'd hoarded our allowances, often taking on extra chores for payment so that we could go riding together. My horse is my one luxury, some like Arty say, shaking their heads at what they see as money wasted, especially sinful when money is as tight as it often is for me. My horse is not a luxury, though; for me, he is a necessity, a need as real as water, food and space. In or out of work, I have somehow managed to keep my horse by cleaning stalls, grooming, teaching and training without ever accepting a penny's loan from anyone.

"You'll give Cherokee a hug for me, won't you?" Rick asks.

"Sure, honey, a big hug. And a carrot." It always makes me happy when my brother remembers to mention my horse.

"Good. Well, have a nice ride." He smiles a sweet, heartfelt smile, maybe remembering the days we used to ride trails together, riding and talking with the unthinking ease that comes with sharing thousands of hoof-miles.

"Yeah, Rick, I will," I say, rising and straightening the strap of my 10-pound shoulder bag. "See you soon. Take care now. You too, Ma."

Blowing them both kisses, I give his left foot, encased in a clean white tube sock, a farewell squeeze as he looks at Mother. He remains silent for a moment, tasting the sweetness of his news once again.

"They think I can come home soon, Ma. My temp has to stay down for a little while longer, that's all." He pauses, gazing at her. "I could come home, at least for now."

She looks into his eyes, seeing only him now, oblivious to my leave-taking. Rick can come home soon and that's what matters; the gift of a few more days or weeks or months of time when he sits with her in her kitchen, wearing rubber gloves, chopping vegetables; when he listens to Big Band jazz with her, laughing in recognition of the old songs; when they sit together on the worn green family room couch, watching old movies on TV; when he is there — there for her in a way that no one — especially Arty — has ever been, except for maybe my real father, from whom I get my very dark eyes, hair and my occasional but bottomless, dark moods. After all these years I no longer miss him or feel his loss. It's been so long that I don't remember my father clearly any more, except for unexpected and infrequent moments when the smell of Prince Albert pipe tobacco or the sight of a red plaid woolen hunting jacket pulls me back to a crystalline glimpse of him, vanishing at once and I find myself, unaccountably, in tears.

This is a special, private moment for Rick and Mother and I leave, hearing my ma say, "That's wonderful! When? Tomorrow? In the morning? I'll make us such a nice dinner. I'll roast a turkey with dressing. Oh honey, I'm so glad." Her voice quivers with feeling.

"Yeah," I hear him say as the door silently, slowly starts its swing shut. "That would be great, with the sweet potatoes." His voice rises in enthusiasm. "And maybe we can start to get the holiday things up from the basement. Julie will be home and I want to really dress up the house for her this Christmas. I saw a wreath last year with a great Art Deco look and it would be terrific on the front door. It was in one of those specialty boutiques. Even if they don't still have it, I'll bet they could order it."

The sounds of my riding boots echo down the scrubbed hallway.

January, 1986 — ELIXIR OF LOVE

"Do you still have a gun?" my brother says, using his real voice as he asks me to kill him. He speaks in that voice, the tone he used years ago to tell Julie she should always dress warmly in the cold weather — the one he spoke with when he wrapped his scarf around her little girl neck and told her he loved her — the voice telling me, many months ago, "I have AIDS."

"What? What are you saying?" I look desperately around the room for an open door or window, any way out of the situation I have secretly dreaded for months.

"Why do you want to know?" I answer, trying to stall for time; I feel my heart racing, my face flushing and sweat forming on my forehead.

"Lucy, it's not going to get better." He sits up in bed, running his fingers through hair now prematurely white from chemotherapy, once black like mine. He is 37.

"Don't say that. We have to hope." I hate myself as soon as I say those words, spoken in a phony voice reserved for social occasions. Years of being a reporter have taught me the difference between a real voice and all the others. We recognize our own real voices, not our job or social voices, or even those we normally use with our families and friends; they surprise our adult selves when we hear them, since we have become so used to speaking in certain ways and have learned this from the time we started talking.

"Don't talk like that!" our parents reprimand, drilling us in language that hides rather than expresses.

We also recognize the real voice of another. Maybe it's an untaught skill, an animal instinct left in us. An authentic voice commands our total attention when we hear it, sometimes causing goose flesh, so real and basic are the emotions expressed.

Since Rick has been ill, so much of what had been real about me has been numbed by fear, not only of the daily losses but of future grief. Most of the few genuine moments in my life when I have found the courage, trust and voice to speak directly from my heart have been with Rick and occasionally, Julie; but during last month's brief visit, my daughter treated me as a polite stranger might. I sometimes wonder if I will ever find my real voice again.

My hands work nervously on a piece of cross-stitching that will become an embroidered pillow of Don Quixote, one Rick designed after Picasso's print of Sancho and the Don. I'm not sure who will get it when I'm done, but the embroidery with its tiny measured steps, over and over, helps me stay calm. Rick says he finds it soothing to watch my needle go up, crossing over and down, then up again and crossing over. When I sit with him and sew, he needs less medication, maybe because of the steady rhythm of the work, maybe because of the camaraderie.

"I know you have the pistol. Use it on me, please." His dark eyes shine in the afternoon's shadows. There are no lights on in his room. I work my way through this embroidery more by feel than sight, but can see well enough to catch the tears in Rick's eyes. Half-finished drawings are scattered at the foot of his bed.

"Stop it, Rick," I say sharply, hoping to stem the direction of this talk.

"Why not?" He continues. "It's the best way. We can make it look like an accident — like I was downstairs in the garage, cleaning it."

"Stop it!" It is painful to breathe. The abrupt tightening in my chest makes me look away to the snow-covered power lines outside, so like my frost-encrusted freezer but without its deadly contents.

"Please, Lucy, you're the only one I can trust to do it. It's awful to die like this." His tall, thin frame looks frail against the blue-white sheets.

"I can't, Rick. It's not right."

"What do you mean? This is beyond right and wrong." He glares, but I stare him down.

"It's *not* right and you know what I mean! I can't take your life. Nothing you can say will change that," I answer, a note of anger sharpening my tone, regretfully.

"Why not? What's it worth now, anyway?"

"Everything, damn you, your life's worth everything." I can't keep my eyes from misting over. "Don't you see?"

It's bad enough to know I'll be without him, missing him the rest of my life, but to be the one who brings it about, willfully, prematurely — the one who literally blows him away from this life — I don't know how I could live knowing I'd done that. I'd have to kill myself, too.

"What? Are you afraid you'll be arrested? I told you, we'll make it look like an accident. Just help me hold the gun to my head in case my hand shakes. I'm scared to do it alone. Please, I want you to be with me on this."

"No!" I've thought he might ask me to do this and have wrestled the issue inside myself for months, always returning to the same basic, heartfelt conclusion that life — the lives of other people, not necessarily my own — was precious. There are still times when I automatically see others' lives as so much more valuable than mine.

"I thought you loved me!" He's turning angry now, yelling and impatiently flipping his hair out of his eyes with a flinging hand, off his feverish forehead, toward his left temple, the temple closest to me, the one I would bring the gun to.

"It isn't the cops or what you mean to me or anything like that. Damn you, Rick, you ought to know how much you mean to me." I stop for a moment, trying to catch my breath. "Even without laws, without anybody else ever knowing, it's just not right. Your life is not mine to take. That's all I know." I'm too exhausted from this to know anything else.

"You sound like a catechism." His mouth is a thin, bitter line. He looks away to the dresser, to the picture of us taken two years ago. In it, we're both laughing, our arms around each other. We look so much younger.

"Maybe I do sound like one. I don't care. All I really know is that I can't do it." By now, I am slumped down in the old rocker, sobbing, rocking faster and faster, my embroidery thrown on the rug like an old cleaning rag.

Rick's face is red. "You don't love me enough to do it. That's what you're saying!" He turns away from me, his voice a mixture of rage and tears.

Mother opens the door and sticks her head in the bedroom doorway, concern marking her face. "What's going on in here?" Cowboy walks in quietly beside her, sinking down next to my rocker, resting his head on his right paw.

"What does it look like?" Rick indicates me with an incline of his head. "Lucy's crying," he mumbles, gripping the satin border of the royal blue blanket.

"I can see that," she says sharply, waiting expectantly for more explanation.

He sits up straighter in bed, facing the tall, pale woman with carelessly arranged dark hair. "It's my fault. I upset her."

"Shut up, Rick," I say, still sniffling, reaching for the embroidery. I can't stand this.

"No, it is, it's my fault," he says, trying to meet my eyes with his own. "Lucy, I'm sorry."

"God damn you, Rick!" I'm so furious with him, I get up to leave, almost stumbling out of the chair and tripping over the dog, who quickly moves to a safer distance.

Mother intervenes. She feels wounded, personally rejected if people fight with Rick in his weakened state and try to go away mad, though she used to act that way herself with him until his diagnosis. "Lucy, don't leave. Whatever it is, he's sorry. What could be so awful you have to leave?" A long silence settles as I stand, half leaning against the dresser and concentrating on the worn hem of my jeans and the clean lavender laces in my white sneakers. Rick's chest heaves with more than his usual effort to breathe.

"I asked her to kill me."

"Oh, my God!" Mother moans and her voice catches in the back of her throat as the sobs start and her hands fly to her chest.

"Don't worry. I told him I couldn't," I say, trying to reassure her.

"But to even think it, to ask you." Mother sinks into the wing chair on the opposite side of Rick's bed, with muffled, choking sounds, her chin pressed tightly into her chest, chapped hands twisting her apron, the one with faded chickens that I gave her years ago, the one she wears from dawn to bedtime, sometimes over slacks and a top, sometimes over a slip. Today, she wears it over a blue pants suit.

"How could you?" she hisses at him. She wipes the corner of her right eye with the edge of the washed-out cloth.

"Ma, stop it," I say. "I can see how he could ask. I just can't do it and he never should have told you." I know my mother hates to show tears and cries only in the most extreme situations. My stomach lurches when Mother cries.

"What — are you in on this with him," she attacks, using the energy to slow the flow of tears.

"For God's sake, there's nothing to be in on. He asked and I said no." I lean forward toward Mother, tension locking my legs.

"I should hope so!" She raises her voice to a shrill yell. "How can you even stand here and discuss it so calmly?"

I am not calm. My legs and hands are trembling and I'm still blowing my nose loudly as I ease myself back in the rocker, reaching for the comfort of my embroidery and its neat rows of cross-stitching.

"Stop it with her, Ma. I told you it was my fault." Rick's face is pale with seriousness.

"Of course it was!" Mother's chin juts aggressively at him. "My God, suicide. You'd burn in Hell forever, Rick, and that's not enough, you'd take her with you. How can you even talk that way?" His face flushes, but from guilt or spiking fever I can't tell. He looks to me, mutely asking for support.

"Ma, let him alone. He's sick, for God's sake," I say, a warning tone in my voice.

"He's sick? Of course he's sick." The washed-out apron looks as though it might tear under her twisting fingers. "Who should know it better than me? I take care of him!" Mother lets a hint of righteous self pity enter her tone, hoping to remind us of her sacrifices.

"And you never let anyone forget it, either." I grip the embroidery hoop, feeling its smooth, cool metal against my hot hands. "You'd think you were the only one who takes him to the clinic or sits with him and keeps him company and reads to him and gets him a snack or fresh pajamas —"

"Stop it, both of you!" Rick leans forward, interrupting us with his force. Cowboy snaps to attention, snarling low in his throat, warning us all.

Falling back on the pillows, wearied from this outburst, Rick says, "Lucy, really, I'm sorry." The dog settles back on his haunches, still watchful.

"I know." Pale and frightened, My brother sinks deeper into the bed. Mother turns on the lights, giving us both an angry look. She leaves, blowing her nose loudly with one of the used, wadded-up, ancient tissues kept in her apron pocket.

Rick's voice is low. "I'm just so tired of everything. The pain and the shots. The lousy friends who haven't called in months. Tired, just tired."

"I know." Even two small words are an effort.

"No, you don't," he says without anger or malice, but as a simple statement of fact. "You can't know."

"I try."

Once again, he looks at the photo on his dresser, which he framed with an ornate Art Deco creation in silver and brass. My copy at home is double-matted, with a plain chrome frame. The crystal vase I gave him fills my eyes with pleasure, exquisitely complementing that picture in its simplicity.

Dancing to the End . . . .

This past December, just six weeks ago, I'd disgraced myself by bursting into tears in the better crystal section of Marshall Field's housewares department. The money I'd been saving to buy Rick a vase had vanished. I'd searched all through my purse, but it was gone, along with my wallet and credit cards. They could have been taken at any of several places that day — the news room, the library, anywhere.

The vase sat on its sparkling glass shelf, facing me, an iris engraved on its surface, the memory of that design engraving itself into my mind.

"It's not you; it's not Fields," I'd said to the worried-looking sales clerk, tears running down my face. "It's just that I wanted to get him something really nice, that vase, but I've lost the money and this is probably his last Christmas — never mind," I'd said, aiming myself toward the escalator. Appalled, Maureen repeatedly tried to loan me the money. After numerous offers I'd finally agreed. Only for Rick.

"Marry me, Lucy, please," he says to me. "I'm so alone."

"Marry you?" Unlike his plea for mercy killing, this surprises me, coming as it does, seemingly out of nowhere.

"Yes. After all, we've talked about it off and on for years. God knows, we love each other. Really, Lucy, marry me."

"Oh, honey, no. I don't think so." From time to time, we've sat together, nursing broken hearts from spent romances, discussing the idea of marriage but never seriously.

"Christ, it's not like we're really brother and sister!" Rick flips his hair from his eyes impatiently. "Dammit Lucy, how much longer do I have? My job's gone, my friends, too. It could be my last chance to have a normal life, to be like other people, straight people. We could stand together in church and look them all in the eye and I could be like —"

"Like what? Who? The people who don't respect us or anyone else who doesn't fit their mold?"

"Oh, Christ, you won't help me kill myself while I still can and you won't make the rest of my life easier by marrying me — you just don't give a damn!"

"You bastard, how you can say that —" My teeth clench with anger.

"Get out of here," Rick says. "Why do you bother sitting here, anyway? Go visit your girlfriend!" I recoil from the sound of him smashing his fist into the headboard of the old maple bed and Cowboy, on alert, bounds to his feet with a short, sharp bark.

"Will you shut up? You know I care and I choose to be with you right here, right now, the way I did Tuesday and last week and the way I'll choose to be here for a whole bunch of tomorrows! But that's different from killing you or marrying you. What is this shit, 'Lucy, prove your love to me' day?"

He looks down, shaking his head, embarrassed. "No, that's not it," he says, meeting my eyes. "Let me feel I can take care of you. Please." He takes a deep breath, steadying himself. "Listen Lucy, Julie could have a real father again. Haven't I helped you raise her?"

He has in so many ways, the memories of those times moving me to an overwhelming tenderness for him. "You've been my rock, honey," I say as gently as I can. "But even if they fight, Ed's still her dad."

He sighs, his voice trembling. "She's like my daughter, the only little girl I've ever had. I miss her. I miss taking her to the movies when she was little or that night three winters ago you were caught in a blizzard and I drove over and stayed with her. We played gin rummy half the night, trying to keep each other from worrying about you driving in that snow."

Dancing to the End   . . . .

His eyes fill so that he pauses, blinking. "Remember last year when she helped me cook your birthday dinner and surprise you? She had me hold the ladder while she put up streamers."

He stops for breath. "She only spent a couple of days with us at Christmas." I wipe his tears with a corner of the sheet, grieving that she stayed at Ed's the rest of the time.

"Rick, it's not that she doesn't love you or doesn't want to be with you. She's really not deserting you, honey. She's just so scared — petrified."

"Of what? Of catching it and dying? By being in the same room, for God's sake?"

I find myself falling into Maureen's habit, looking down and shaking my head when confronted with intense emotion. "Rick, Rick, Rick," I say, "No, honey, of course not. She's terrified of losing you, the way we all are. She's just young and thinks she can run from fear by not being here. She doesn't know any better."

He looks at me, brightening. "At least we got to celebrate her eighteenth birthday while she was here. Congrats, sis. Don't ever worry about her being taken away from you, not ever again." We share a look, needing no more words on this.

Shaking my head again, I recall the days and weeks, months and years lived in fear of losing my only child because of who and what I am. The secrecy of my life. All those times Rick stood by me, steadying my confidence, cheering me up, counseling courage and endurance in a prying world eager to label me unfit until my daughter's eighteenth birthday.

In the past, Julie's resentment of Ed outweighed her growing discomfort with my lifestyle? — with me? — so that she lived with me throughout her school years. Now, despite the persistent animosity she feels toward her father and his second family, she chooses to be away from me.

Rick sighs. "She's 18 and an adult. But she still needs us. You always said I was more her father than Ed was."

"I meant it. If it hadn't been for you, I don't know how I could have gotten her this far or me either, for that matter." The clarity of this truth hits me with a force that makes me pause, reaching over to touch his arm. "And honestly, I can't imagine Julie ever having a better dad than you."

"But you won't marry me." His mouth compresses bitterly. He examines the reddened knuckles of his right hand.

"It isn't you, Rick. And this has nothing to do with Maureen. I never liked being married. You know that. I guess some people are more cut out for marriage." For a moment, I imagine Rick as my husband — at least in name, with society's sanctions and congratulations — but shake my head with resolve. "Once was enough. No more marriage."

He takes a deep breath but it's an easier sigh, not nearly so bitter and angry. "We still look good together — even now." He takes my hand firmly in both of his. Cowboy lies down by my chair but keeps his eyes open.

"I know. We're a great-looking couple." We look at each other and smile, hearing the afternoon opera that Ma turned on. She says the Sunday opera helps her know it's Sunday, helps her relax. The music ends and the announcer tells them the next portion of "The Elixir of Love" will be broadcast after a brief intermission. Mother sticks her head into the doorway. "Are you two still fighting?" Her eyes remain wet and red.

"We weren't fighting, Ma, you were fighting."

"Don't start with me again, Rick, I'm telling you, don't start." Her hands are on her hips, braced and defiant.

He beams like a small boy presenting the project he's made for her in fifth grade woodworking class. "I'm not starting anything." He lets a long moment pass silently for emphasis. "I just asked Lucy to marry me."

Ma's shoulders rise, her face brightens and that wonderful, broad smile lifts her. Joy overcomes the disappointment and fatigue that have marked her 58-year-old face and she is once again a beautiful woman. "Well, now you're talking! That would be wonderful, for the family, for you, for everyone!" she says, squeezing Rick's arm. Turning, she yells downstairs, "Arty! Arty, are you sleeping by the TV? Get up here. Rick asked Lucy to marry him. Isn't that something? Arty!" She steps forward and looks at me expectantly.

"For God's sake, Ma, don't make such a big thing of it. I already said no." Since my divorce in 1973, I've consistently tried to stop her attempts to link me once again with a man, but without success. Mother will not rest until she sees me "settled down again with someone nice — a man."

"What do you mean, you already said no? It's a big thing and you should think about it. Arty? Arty, come here. Just 'cause you shoveled the driveway and tired yourself out doesn't mean you're going to sleep all afternoon, does it?" Her voice takes on a tone of need, of urgency.

Arty shuffles in, wearing his favorite old slippers. Two new pairs still sit in their boxes, stacked neatly in his closet. "Rae, did you say marriage?" He yawns, looking at Ma, now small and disheveled in the large arm chair. Arty's voice softens. "It's Sunday, Rae Ann. Take off the apron." He likes to see Mother look less disorganized on Sundays, the day he views as a time for gathering thoughts together neatly before starting another week.

A withering look from Ma. "Never mind the apron, Arty. Rick asked Lucy to marry him."

"And?" His white eyebrows arch toward the golf cap on his head. He claims it keeps his bald head warm. The argyle pattern on it matches his cardigan sweater. Any time now, he will sigh mightily.

"And nothing," I say with a deeply drawn breath. It gives me satisfaction to sigh first. "You know how I feel about marriage." I watch Arty sigh, sinking deeply into a matching wing chair to the left of Mother's. He looks at his son who looks away, toward the cloth I am embroidering with mechanical movements.

He sighs again, staring at me with intense, pale blue eyes. "Now tell me what this has to do with your past marriage. Just tell me that."

"Nothing. Absolutely nothing."

"Exactly. So put away your feelings about that. Look at this with an open mind. You know this would benefit the family, with the both of you married like normal people —"

My closed mind shrivels into itself as I curl deeply into the rocker for protection, setting my cross-stitching on my lap. I speak slowly, clearly, marshalling my logic. "Arty, I never should have married in the first place. We all know that. We know how things turned out with Ed and me. But I did and certainly don't regret having Julie."

"She's the only good thing to come out of that marriage," Mother interrupts, "even though she's away now."

Away for now? Forever? "How could I even consider a second marriage? Isn't one mistake enough?" I continue.

The doorbell rings several times over the sound of "Elixir of Love," followed by a new melody, Aunt Alice's "Hello. I'm here. I'm here at 1835 Lawn Street. Hel-looo." She slams the door closed behind her.

"We know where we live, Alice, thank you," Arty says. "Please take off your boots and don't track in snow." He is tired from shoveling, preferring to sleep through the afternoon in front of the TV.   There are also the decades of friction between him and his sister-in-law, who so fiercely protects what she sees as her side of the family's best interests.

"Well, I'm just trying to make a pleasant entrance, Arty. You don't have to be like that."

Aunt Alice strides in, bringing with her small gusts of Emeraude and concern as she glances critically at Mother's washed-out apron and disarrayed hair, saying nothing. At 62, Alice looks many years younger than Mother, who is her baby sister. My aunt is a delicate refinement of my mother's even, but slightly coarser features.   Alice gently smooths her shoulder-length page boy, dyed bright red and regards Arty with an injured look. "You don't have to be so nasty; you know that, Arty."

"Yes, he does," mumbles Rick.

"That's enough," Mother says.   A seasoned and wily contender, she knows better than to waste her strength on side issues when there is a major confrontation at hand.

Cowboy gets up and goes to Alice, who absent-mindedly pats his head.

"So, how is everything," Aunt Alice asks, getting right to the point. Unlike me, some in the family have become more authentic since Rick's diagnosis. Not that Alice has ever been shy about making her opinions known. In fact, she has a way of walking into rooms, conversations, even relationships and taking over. She throws a smile in Rick's direction, revealing perfect, even teeth. "Feeling any better?"

"Not really. The doctor says he'll be trying something new this week." He looks down, fingering the edge of the blanket, sorry to disappoint her.

"What doctor?"

"Dr. Ziti."

"You remember, Alice, the one you don't like." Mother can't resist.

"Of course I remember, Rae Ann. There is nothing wrong with my memory." She discovers a thread and picks it from her tailored turquoise jacket. She opens her tan leather bag. Flipping open an ebony compact, she first checks her flawless makeup in the mirror, then scrutinizes Rick. Her favorite, she often favors him over her own sister. "Well, you look better than last week," she pronounces gravely. If she has spoken, that's the way it is, according to Alice.

Arty rises and moves an armless, wooden chair with an upholstered seat toward Alice, on Mother's right-hand side, saying, "Dr. Ziti says he's going to try something that's still in the experimental stage. He thinks it's very promising."

"And he's thought that before," Ma reminds him. "I get tired of Dr. Ziti-this, Dr. Ziti-that. Sometimes I feel like we live according to what he says. One week it's this, the next week, that. Whatever the great Dr. Ziti says, we do. We're completely under his control."

"I remember him when he was little Donny Ziti down the block." Arty sits in his chair, ignoring Ma's frustration. "His father comes to me and says, 'Donny's short for his age, Arty, but a real go-getter. There's nothing he'd like more than to be on your team. Give him a chance. It would mean a lot to him and he'll do a good job for you, you'll see.' So I did. I gave him a chance. And he was the best little catcher I ever had on a team."

Rick starts to say something. My hand on his arm stops him. In my memory I see my brother, sitting at home alone during all the years his father was out coaching other people's boys. Arty used to say Rick threw like a girl. Arty sits back, sighing and smiling, seeming to enjoy his son's pained expression. "Little Donny Ziti. And look at him now."

"Right, a fine young doctor, my *short,* fine young doctor," Rick says sarcastically.

"Well, he's the best of the lot, don't you think? I don't like his personality but you seem to have done pretty well with him so far," Alice says, focusing her luminous, sea-colored eyes on Rick, encircling him with the warmth of her smile. A surge of affection for her swells up inside me.

"I have to admit it, he seems competent, Aunt Alice." Rick relents in the face of her charm, as do so many.

"I just hope he is," Mother chimes in. "Something has to make up for his bossiness. He's just one arrogant S.O.B."

"Doctors are like that a lot. What counts is skill," Arty says smugly.

Aunt Alice twirls a long red strand of hair around her forefinger. "Arty, doctors have disappointed me, God knows. First it was this test, then it was that test, then something else and they never knew anything anyway. But I know it must be cancer — eating out my ovaries, my bladder, my intestines — all my insides. I know, because they protrude out my privates. The doctors laughed, so I almost gave up on them, but the pain I get when I go to the bathroom! For 25 years, I've endured this. I could die in a minute." She stops, snapping her finger for emphasis. "Just like that — right now even. You don't know."

Alice has outlived four of her doctors, all of them younger than she is, but she frequently reminds us she has been at

144

death's weathered door for over 20 years. Rick and I try not to laugh at her, but it's hopeless. We catch each other's eye, breaking into laughs bordering on snorting guffaws, reveling in the release, with tears threatening to spill over. Cowboy, back at my feet, lifts his head, looking from Rick to me.

"That's enough, both of you," Mother interjects. You know my sister's not well. Even when we were little girls, our mother used to say she was the delicate one."

"That's right," Alice is quick to agree. "That dreadful pneumonia I used to get every winter. My God, how many times it almost killed me! Rae used to bring me hot lemonade when I was sick. She would stay until she saw me drink every drop." Her voice softens.

The two sisters exchange a fond glance, then look down, embarrassed, as Alice takes Mother's hand in her own.

Mother raises her head, smiling. "Rick's asked Lucy to marry him." Alice's eyes open wide. Mother turns, locking her gaze on me.

I sew without looking, prick my left index finger and swear, "Shit!" pressing the tiny puncture with my thumbnail, watching the red dome of blood expand.

"Lucy, this marriage could be a good thing for you both," Mother says, ignoring the language as well as the needle prick. "You could be like a family — you and Rick, normal. Like husband and wife."

"I always thought we were a family," I throw back, bloody finger in my mouth.

"That's not what I mean and you know it." Mother's voice cuts. Alice looks at her in silence. Arty looks like he's dying to cut in but stays silent.

I take a deep breath and resume stitching with a vengeance. "What exactly do you mean?"

"A family. You and Rick marry like regular people. You sell your house and come live here with us. We'd all be together."

I sigh, glancing down at another completed row of neat cross stitching. "Is it that you need more help? Is that it? You need me to come over more? Should we think about my spending a night or two here every week or so to give you some time off?"

I hate to take on any more though, since I'm rarely home enough to do more than yard work, get my mail and phone messages, sleep and empty the garbage. My poems are written on the run in precious moments snatched from tasks at work, errands and visits to Rick, often existing for months on envelopes, scrap paper and the backs of memos before they make it into the word processor. My only "relaxation" at home is whatever time I make to work on my poetry. When I'm too tired to write, I try getting through a few chapters of the book I'm reading at the time. Propped up on pillows in bed until my eyelids droop, I regretfully turn off the light, sometimes too tired even to think of Maureen or murmur a brief prayer for Rick and Julie before sinking into sleep.

"It's not the work," Mother insists. Rick closes his eyes, not in fatigue, but in embarrassment. His face is bright red.

"Well, you certainly never let anyone forget it," I answer, sewing faster, trying to concentrate my anger on the shifting light reflected on the needle as it moves through the cloth.

"Don't talk that way to my sister. She's been through more than you can know, widowed out of the blue when you were only eight!" Aunt Alice is now her champion.

"Lucy, why are you so stubborn? You're my only child; I only want what's best for you. As Rick's wife, there would be benefits — it could make things easier for you financially."

I realize I'm grinding my teeth. "It could be all the right things for all the wrong reasons." My voice is starting to rise, casting aside the logical lines of defense, going for the ethical. "It wouldn't be honest, for God's sake!" I jam the thick embroidery needle through the thin fabric.

"Stop talking like that," Arty snorts.

"Lucy, Lucia, it's not like you're blood-related brother and sister." Mother persists with the factual approach as she unfolds the wad of tissue in her lap.

"Look, Ma, blood-related or not, the fact of the matter is that with two gay people —"

"I don't ever want to hear that!" Aunt Alice interrupts. Her hair whirls wildly as she faces Mother, gripping her hand. "How can you let them say that?"

"What do you want from me? They're free to say what they like."

"That'll be the day," Rick mumbles.

I shift my gaze to Alice, gathering the threads of my argument, presenting them to the one family member I count on for sanity under pressure. "Aunt Alice, look at the facts. I mean, two gay people marrying —"

"The Hell with the facts, Lucy!" She slices the air around her with her hand as though writing. "It would make a great obituary: 'He leaves behind his devoted wife, Lucia and his loving daughter, Julie.' "

"That's enough, Alice! Shut up!" Mother leans forward, looking for a moment like she might slap her own sister's face in front of us all. My needle remains poised in the air in mid-stitch. Arty sits, pale in the big chair, momentarily stunned into silence. Cowboy moves warily to his feet.

"No, you shut up, Rae! You want people to know? You want them to talk more than they already do? The whole neighborhood's been whispering about those two kids of yours for years, only now it's worse. You're my sister and how do you think this has been for *me,* having to live here, holding my head high above the stories and rumors of not one, but two homosexuals in the family? What better thing than marriage — between the both of them yet!"

I throw the embroidery to my lap, furious with the one I thought would be sensible. "It would just be for show. It wouldn't be an honest-to-God marriage, Aunt Alice."

"Never mind! It's the show that counts — and what people remember."

"And you want them to remember a lie." I can't believe this. Of Arty and Ma, yes, but not Alice.

"Better a lie than a scandal, Lucy!" She twirls a red ringlet frantically.

Arty sighs deeply and bores his watery blue eyes at me. "So is it a lie that you love Rick, that you care about him?"

"Of course not!"

"So you love him and he loves you." He pauses, presumably for maximum effect. "Does that make your marriage a lie?"

"You know how things are and what we are. We don't love each other in a marriage way."

Rick leans toward me, his face only a foot from mine. "That wouldn't make it any less of a marriage. It wouldn't mean we don't love each other. And we wouldn't be so alone."

"He's right. Listen to your brother," Ma tells me. Gently, I release Rick's grip but can't avoid his eyes.

"It could only be for the best. And the — personal business between you two — well, that's nobody's business." Aunt Alice is trying to use words with discretion.

"Oh, but we'd be marrying because you seem to think it is everybody's business!" I throw back, unable to keep my voice from breaking, from hurt as much as rage.

"Lucy, why are you so stubborn? We would make you such a nice wedding — nothing large, just tasteful and intimate, for the immediate family and a few friends," Aunt Alice says. "It could be the wedding you never had, with flowers and a couple of bridesmaids and pretty dresses." Aunt Alice gestures into the air with her outstretched fingers, creating the scene of a picture postcard wedding.

Ready to cry again, I think of my elopement 18 years ago; the failed marriage to Ed; the loss, perhaps permanent, of Julie. "Nothing can change what's past," I say. "My marriage was bad from the start. Very little's been right with it since."

"Leave the past behind you," Aunt Alice goes on, all charm now, leaning toward me in earnestness. "That business with eloping, no family at the wedding, it's all over now. Believe me, darling, it would be my pleasure to pay for the wedding. Let me make you this gift, please."

"No! Now damn it, stop!"

"Don't swear at your aunt," Arty cuts in, quick to reinforce respect for elders and the inadvisability of refusing gifts, no matter how unwanted.

"Shut up, Arty!" He's the last one I want to hear now.

"She's right, Arty, stay out of it. Women understand these things better than men. This is between women." Aunt Alice, filled with the certainty that she knows what constitutes a woman's issue, sits up to her full height of 5'11", a proud Amazon in a tailored turquoise suit, challenging him.

"Please remember where you are, Alice," the small man sputters with anger. "This is my house and you are welcome in it only because you are my wife's sister —"

"Arty, that is *one* thing you're right about. I am your wife's sister. Her family. Her blood relation!"

"What, I can't speak in my own house? You interrupt me? I'm only trying to talk reasonably. Someone here has to." He briefly examines the buttons on his sweater as he recovers from the wound. "She should marry him —"

"You seem to have it all figured out, don't you, Arty," I snarl, my needlework still idle on my lap as I focus on him.

"Now *you* interrupt me!" No playing with buttons now, just the full heat of his wrath falling on me.

"Well, excuse me." Sarcasm saturates my voice. "You, however, seem to have no reservations at all about planning my life for me — with or without my consent." My face feels as red and hot as the bundle of dried chili peppers hanging in my kitchen at home.

"Lucy, we're only thinking of what's best." Aunt Alice is trying to return to the subject at hand, her red hair swinging and covered with greenish globes, reflections of the green-shaded light from the overhead fixture.

"That's right. You know I hate to say it, but I have to agree with your aunt on this," Arty sighs deeply.

"If only you hadn't met that damn Ed your first year at college, with him getting you in trouble and no proper wedding — no wonder you're marriage-shy," Mother says. "It's made your luck bad ever since, 'cause you know God punishes wrongs. If you had listened to us in the past —" Count on Mother to bring up old issues.

"Don't say that, Rae." Arty whirls to confront her with his reddening face. "You'll just make her mad again. Now be quiet about that." He turns to me. "Do it. Just go ahead and do it. Make us all happy and you'll make yourself happy, too. You'll see."

"After all, you can never know from one day to the next; we could all die tomorrow," Aunt Alice reminds me, leaning back into the hard chair as she nods solemnly.

"Even Ed would understand this," Mother says. "I never liked him, he was a lousy son-in-law, he never respected me or Arty, but this, even Ed would see the good in it. You don't have to live so alone, you know. If only you would listen —" She leans forward, trying to lessen the space separating her from me, her only natural child.

Too angry to talk, I stuff my embroidery in my tote bag, ready to walk out.

"See now, Rae Ann, you've got her mad, she's leaving." Arty's half lifted from his chair by exasperation.

"Lucy, you're my daughter; don't leave. You know we love you. Just have some faith in us."

Faith. The term "a crisis of faith" returns to me from my Catholic childhood, referring to the horrible spiritual doubts faced during "a dark night of the soul." When he was hurt and angry, Ed used to say I had no faith in him but it wasn't that. It wasn't personal. I had little or no faith in anything and not much has changed since then. This stops me cold.

The large room is quiet. Cowboy's ears twitch almost audibly in the deep stillness. Rick speaks softly, breaking the silence and turning to face me directly. "Don't go. This isn't about marriage." I cautiously move my weight back into the rocker, surprised and waiting. "I'm sorry now I even brought it up and I'll never ask you again," he says, pausing. "And it's not about asking you to put your life on hold for me, either. It's not about waiting 'til I'm gone —" This is hard for him and I can't help him. "It's about what we are to each other and what we've meant —" He glances down briefly but raises his eyes to meet mine again. "What I mean to you.

Now. For always. What we are together." A deep breath. The worst is over. "I think all the rest of this marriage stuff is just crap, avoiding the main issue."

"You sound like your shrink talking," Arty shoots back.

"Yeah, Dad, and he probably can't hit a long line drive either, so that really puts him at the bottom of your list, right down there with me, like always."

"Stop talking bullshit." Arty sulks, his lower lip thrust forward.

For a long moment, no one speaks. Rick ignores Arty and looks at me, locking my eyes with his and asking quietly, "I need to know." There is no sound except his breathing.

Memory floods my senses, filling the stillness, recalling other silences: the long, accusing stare of the high school counselor, contemptuous of my rumored bent, suspected but never proven and so alien to his narrow, official view of "normal"; that fleeting moment, preserved forever in the amber of memory, when I glimpsed my child's face, realizing it had become an adult's; the time I faced my parents, hearing the clock ticking, the kitchen faucet dripping as I shared the true story of my marriage's death, of who and what I am, where my passions lay and how I live.

From the depths of those memories my real voice rises now, unshaken and enduring, breaking this unbearable silence as I reach for my brother's hand.

"You are my dear one," I say, breathing deeply, without effort, and his dark eyes soften in relief.

February, 1987 — POSTSCRIPT

"Why are you crying? What is it?" she asks, concern knotting her brow as she steps toward me. The tears stream down my face. Wordlessly, I shove the card at her. There's a watercolor painting of a rainbow on the front. Inside it says, "Stay strong, no matter what. We never know what tomorrow may bring."

I found it as I was browsing through the cards in Chicago's feminist book store for women and children. Next to the areas labeled "birthday" and "friendship" was a new category that captured my complete attention: "for the seriously ill." I knew what that meant. There were six or eight cards in this new line, all with messages of loving support and faith, each decorated with pastel drawings and water colors of landscapes.

"If only," I cry to her, "if only these had been around for Rick —" I pause for a moment, taking in air through my mouth. "Now there's special support groups for AIDS patients, their families, partners, loved ones — all kinds, all over the place. We've even got The Quilt on tour, with people paying attention, things getting done. But Rick's not here for any of it." Snuffling, I search my purse blindly for a tissue, groping through wallet, breath mints, tampons, appointment book, car keys, hand lotion, note pads and pens.

"We were all alone and all he had and sometimes it was so damned hard. I tried. I couldn't marry him and he understood that but I tried to be there for him in every other way."

Maureen nods, her hand on my arm. "And you were, Lucy, you were. You were everything to him you could be, everything he could possibly ask for. He knew that. He knew you were with him and would never leave him. That's what counted in the end."

Gulping air, I gasp, "Now I'm the last one left, except for Cowboy. It didn't just kill Rick. It was Ma and Arty, too, grieving themselves to nothing after we lost him. One right after the other, their hearts just broke and gave out. And poor Alice, damn her, feeling she couldn't face people any longer and moving to Las Vegas. One way or another, it did away with us all."

The sobs make it impossible to go on and I'm overcome with anguish and isolation, all alone in a high-wire act; used to be half of a duo, but my brother crashed and burned. Now it takes so much more to go on. Nothing is quite what it seems to be. It never was.

Courage and endurance. Those were the skills Rick and I tried so hard to learn throughout our years together, whether we were trying to grow into our real selves, yet survive in the narrow-minded, punitive environment of a conservative high school; or walking yet another tightrope, discovering, creating who we were and were not, in or out of relationships; or balancing the need to live authentic adult lives against the framework of a society that would seize my child in the name of public morality. Courage, endurance.

I make myself stop crying, telling myself, "You can do it. You've had practice." But I've had too much practice, too many memories. I can't change that, only try to live with it, carrying two letters to help me through the rough times:

February 1, 1986

Dear Rick,

I'm writing because there's no way to tell you, especially without crying all over you. Even writing this, I'm crying now. I know I am going to lose you, that we are going to be separated for eternity and I hate that, no, more than that, I literally cannot abide it. But there is nothing I can do and I sometimes wonder if, egotistically, I don't hate that even more than the loss of you.

This is the hardest letter I've ever had to write.

Though not blood-related, we are blood brother and sister in the Native American sense, bound together because we want to be. Circumstance may have thrown us together but choice has kept us there. What I'm saying is I choose you: the Rick who's been through so much with me; the Rick who's so often pissed me off; the Rick you are now, because sick or not, you're still Rick.

I know the "friends" have disappeared from fear or ignorance, but I'm not better or worse or smarter than they are — just not scared silly. I'm not going to leave you. I not only chose you, again and again, throughout the years; I re-choose you now.

You say it's natural to withdraw from the dying, that it's protection against grief, but if it's true, as you say, that withdrawal means pulling in the love, lessening it bit by bit, I want you to hear me now and know this as surely as you know the texture of your own skin: I won't love you less — I'm going to love you more.

If dying is a natural part of life, let's invest it with all the style and grace we've tried to give everything else. You

155

were never one for the flat or mediocre; it won't happen now. Last July, we went to Fran's "Get in the Spirit" party dressed as 1910 immigrants just off the boat, "in the spirit of our immigrant forebears." We were patched in places but absolutely not mediocre; instead, immaculate and starched, with our slicked-back hair and trimmed mustaches, proud to be searching for new opportunities in a new land. Maybe this transition, painful as it is at times, is a new land to be traveled, too. We have wandered so many paths on uncharted ground together, none of them easy. How hard it was to have gone against the midwestern mainstream, just a couple of mill town kids, born gay enough and smart enough to know we were different and motivated enough to be true to ourselves, no matter what.

It certainly wasn't easy for either of us to bear broken hearts or relationships, but we did, forced on yet another road, screaming, but walking down it just the same; and as we walked, we found more and more of ourselves. I'm sorry we were so filled with grief that we couldn't let much else in for a long time. Let's not do that again. Let's go on gloriously now, in great, flamboyant style, not worrying about the limitations but glorying in the possibilities. This may be our last adventure together; let's make it the best.

Your Lucy

February 3, 1986

My Dearest Lucy,

Your letter means so much — more to me than I can say. I hope I've given you at least a glimpse of how precious you are to me. Don't cry. Even after I'm gone, I'll always be with you, deep inside where no one can ever take me away from you again. Whenever you need me, just listen closely. I'll be there and never desert you.

Your Rick

156